CLIMATE INCORPORATED

When meteorologist Alvin Brook invents a means of controlling the weather, he imagines it will lead to his becoming a world benefactor, with riches for him and his family. Instead, Brook and his wife are murdered, and his invention is stolen and misused by industrialist Marcus Denham. Denham creates the mighty empire of Climate Incorporated, controlling the world's weather and holding nations to ransom ... but he does not anticipate that outraged Nature — and Brook's son — will take their revenge.

*Books by John Russell Fearn
in the Linford Mystery Library:*

THE TATTOO MURDERS
VISION SINISTER
THE SILVERED CAGE
WITHIN THAT ROOM!
REFLECTED GLORY
THE CRIMSON RAMBLER
SHATTERING GLASS
THE MAN WHO WAS NOT
ROBBERY WITHOUT VIOLENCE
DEADLINE
ACCOUNT SETTLED
STRANGER IN OUR MIDST
WHAT HAPPENED TO HAMMOND?
THE GLOWING MAN
FRAMED IN GUILT
FLASHPOINT
THE MASTER MUST DIE
DEATH IN SILHOUETTE
THE LONELY ASTRONOMER
THY ARM ALONE
MAN IN DUPLICATE
THE RATTENBURY MYSTERY

JOHN RUSSELL FEARN

CLIMATE INCORPORATED

Complete and Unabridged

LINFORD
Leicester

First published in Great Britain

First Linford Edition
published 2008

Copyright © 1959 by John Russell Fearn
Copyright © 2004 by Philip Harbottle

British Library CIP Data

Fearn, John Russell, *1908 – 1960*
    Climate incorporated.—Large print ed.—
Linford mystery library
    1. Climatology—Fiction 2. Detective and
mystery stories 3. Large type books
    I. Title
823.9'12 [F]

ISBN 978–1–84782–068–6

Published by
F. A. Thorpe (Publishing)
Anstey, Leicestershire

Set by Words & Graphics Ltd.
Anstey, Leicestershire
Printed and bound in Great Britain by
T. J. International Ltd., Padstow, Cornwall

This book is printed on acid-free paper

1

An idea to change the world

For a long time Alvin Brook had been standing by the window of the lounge, watching the rain. And the longer he watched the grimmer his face became.

'Well, dear, what's the chances? Do we go on that picnic or don't we? Will it clear up?'

Alvin turned, aware of the voice of his wife Nancy. She had just come into the room, a young and pretty woman, but at this moment she was looking a trifle despondent.

'Chances?' Alvin repeated; then he laughed shortly. 'There just aren't any! We're not going on any picnic in this deluge. You can forget all about it.'

Nancy moved over to him and gazed for a while at the raindrops chasing down the window glass. Then she raised her eyes to the weeping gray of the sky.

Expressively she gave a little shiver, and rubbed her bare arms. She was wearing a light summer dress for no other reason than that the calendar said it was June.

'June in name only,' Alvin said, his voice becoming grim. 'This is the third time we've tried to go on a picnic and been spoiled by the weather. Rain, cold winds, and never a glimpse of the sun, except on days when we can't make use of it. It's absolutely idiotic!'

'I agree, but there's absolutely nothing which can be done about it . . . In fact,' Nancy continued, 'I don't know why you didn't foresee a day like this. You're a big noise in the Met office, aren't you? You've got all the charts round you. You said it was going to be fine and warm. Remember all that talk you gave me about anti-something-or-other.'

'Anticyclone, off the Azores,' Alvin mused. 'Yes, it ought to have extended a high pressure ridge and given good weather, but something must have gone wrong. A low-pressure trough has galloped in and upset everything. Don't blame the Met men. That sort of thing's always happening in this haywire climate.'

'Then it's a pity, in this day and age, that something isn't done about it. We can invent H-bombs to destroy whole nations, yet we have to put up with deluges and hurricanes when we expect to get sunburned. David's terribly disappointed. He's sulking in the kitchen over the unpacked picnic basket.'

'Silly lad,' Alvin growled. 'Sulks won't do any good.'

'Then you'd better tell him why they won't. I've pictured you as a hero as far as he is concerned, telling him his marvelous daddy has got it all worked out for sunshine — And look at it!'

Alvin smoldered but said nothing. There were drawbacks — big ones — to being a meteorologist. In some obscure way, according to his family and friends, it made him personally responsible for the weather.

'Play havoc with Sylvia's garden party,' Nancy added, apropos of nothing. 'You told her too that she could rely on sunlight. A nice mess you've made of it!'

Alvin turned and looked at his wife

directly. There was anger and frustration on her usually mild face.

'Look here, Nancy, this is not my fault,' Alvin stated deliberately. 'I can ring up the Met office and have them satisfy you that all the forecast I made last night was correct, as the conditions were then.'

'Some good that would do, with a ruined picnic in front of us and the flowers flattened in the rain. Lord, look at it! Pelting harder than ever . . . we've no chance whatever of having our chicken sandwiches under a hot sun! As a Met man you ought to do something about it.'

'For instance?' Alvin growled. 'Do you think I'm some miracle worker who can stand up and shout 'Cease' to the elements? I'm not. I'm just a human being as disgusted as you are.'

'You mean you're going to sit down to it?'

'That's a pretty idiotic question! What else can I do?'

'I don't know — Hanged if I do.' Nancy hesitated, something like tears coming into her eyes. 'It's all so depressing — so disappointing. I'm sorry if I flared up, Alvin.'

He did not answer. He was staring fixedly at the lashing rain on the window.

'I said I was sorry,' Nancy repeated, laying a hand on his arm. 'Didn't you hear me?'

'Yes — sort of.' Alvin looked at her vaguely. 'Perhaps it's a good thing you blew up. It did something to me.'

'I didn't mean it, honestly.'

'Yes, you did — and I don't blame you one bit . . . You said in so many words that as a Met man I ought to do something about it.'

'Yes, but . . . I spoke without thinking. Naturally you can't do anything. Nobody can.'

'Why can't they?' Alvin moved to the window, hands in pockets, and stared at the rain. Then he swung abruptly to look at Nancy again. 'Yes, why can't they?' he repeated. 'Man has always been at the mercy of the weather, and yet he's conquered everything else except one or two virulent diseases. He's mastered the sea, the air, and the land. Even space! Yet he puts up with rain, hurricane, and fog, tolerates paralysis of cities because he thinks the climate is something too big to handle . . . It isn't, you know. Somebody has to master it, one day.'

Nancy came forward slowly, surprise in her blue eyes. 'Alvin, I never heard you say so much before.'

'I've never been so moved before. Control of the climate is a virgin field which no scientist or meteorologist has ever trodden before . . . suppose Alvin Brook trod it?'

'You — you mean — '

'I mean,' Alvin said, with a grand gesture towards the rain, 'subdue this sort of thing! Find a way to supply the weather that is required. It could be . . . done.'

'But how?'

Alvin smiled a little. 'That is the part that wants thinking about, and I can't think of anybody better placed to do it than myself . . . ' In imagination he suddenly leapt ahead ten years. 'Just think of it, Nancy! Perfectly controlled climate. The assurance that a certain day will be cloudless, together with the assurance that another day will be wet. Think of the difference that would make to our way of living. Think of the farmers, to mention only one body who rely on the weather.'

Nancy looked at the rain on the window, then she gave a little sigh.

'It's a wonderful dream, Alvin, even if it doesn't come true.'

'But it will, dearest. You've started off the spark, and I shan't rest now until I've followed the thing through — Bring David in and let me make a promise to him. That's one way of being sure that I'll keep it.'

Nancy looked doubtful for a moment, but nevertheless she obeyed. In a moment or two she had brought the serious-eyed boy from the kitchen. He looked at his father with undisguised irritation.

'You think I told you wrong last night when I said it was going to be fine, don't you, David?' Alvin asked.

David, ten years old, glanced towards the window, then back to his father.

'It's wet, dad, and you said it was going to be fine.'

'I know. I got it wrong, through a

reason that is too complicated for you to understand. But look, I'm going to make another promise to you, and this time I shall keep it . . . By the time you are a man you are going to be able to have nice weather whenever you want it. So is everybody else. That's a promise.'

'Smashing,' the boy said, shrugging, then with an unusual sagacity, 'How are you going to do it?'

'I'm going to do things with machines, things that will make certain no more picnics will ever be ruined . . . Now, give me a smile, son.'

It was slow in coming, but it came finally. Alvin nodded in approval.

'Good! No more sulking at the weather, David. We'll have our picnic somehow before the summer's finished — but in the meantime we'll have to stay at home today.'

★   ★   ★

Alvin Brook had not been joking. His wife's remarks had started something, the depth of which she had no conception.

8

Alvin patched up the remainder of the miserably wet Sunday as far as he could, then next morning returned to his usual met duties with ideas crowding the back of his mind. That he was preoccupied was immediately apparent to his fellow workers in the chart-lined regions of the met office.

'Have a good weekend, Alvin?' asked Johnson, the senior meteorologist-in-charge.

'Hardly.' Alvin looked at him with frank eyes. 'I was bogged down completely by my own forecast, and I don't think my wife or son have forgiven me even yet.'

'Too bad. Glad it wasn't my weekend off. Hope it behaves better next weekend. I've the garden to fix up.'

Johnson turned to go but Alvin caught at his arm. 'A moment, Frank. What went wrong with the weather yesterday? That Azores anticyclone was building up firmly on Saturday night.'

'That was Saturday,' Johnson sighed. 'Take a look at the chart for yesterday and see what happened . . . ' He signaled to the further wall as he went over to it. Alvin followed him and stood gazing at the huge chart. 'There it is! A small depression, which we thought quite innocuous, suddenly developed and deepened, moving rapidly north eastwards. The whole country was affected. The Midlands worst of all, and bang went one perfectly good forecast.'

'And our name became mud,' Alvin sighed. 'Yet again we took it on the chin.'

Johnson frowned. 'How'd you mean — took it on the chin? We couldn't help the mistake, could we?'

'Of course not. I was just thinking — suppose we'd have been able to steer that depression away, this high pressure area from the Azores would have extended its influence and we've had had glorious sun and a temperature around ninety Fahrenheit.'

'Pipe dreams, m'lad,' Johnson reproved. 'There are two things in this world we've got to put up with — women and the weather. Now get busy on the reports of those Atlantic charts.'

Alvin nodded and turned quietly to his day's work — a routine job of weather-chart analysis, mathematics, computations, and the working out of air pressures, humidity, millibars and isobars.

As he completed various sections of his work it was transferred to another worker; then to the map forecaster; and finally to the radio and television department where the forecasts for various areas were transmitted to the various stations and ships at sea.

In the main it looked like being fine. The Azores anticyclone looked like exerting its real influence. Which was also a bitter irony to Alvin, flogging his brains in the bright sunlight pouring through the window. He worked mechanically, reserving his real concentration for other things. Through the day he managed to appropriate some old weather charts from a cupboard and when the evening came he took them home with him.

What he was doing he did not say, but his wife could draw her own conclusions. She went out shortly after tea for an evening of tennis, whilst David went to a local birthday party. She returned to find Alvin in shirtsleeves, hair rumpled, and an extinguished pipe in his mouth

— whilst all over the table were notes and figures, and on the floor with the ends held down with a pair of shoes were weather charts.

'Busy?' Nancy asked, rather dryly, and she received a reply that was something like 'Umph.'

'David not back yet?' she inquired, and after looking at her for a long minute Alvin answered:

'It's the hot and cold air problem every time. Get that sorted out and things can be done. Repulse cold or hot air at will.'

Nancy laid aside her white pullover as she considered.

'Are you talking about your job, or your dream?' she asked finally.

'How d'you mean?'

'I mean, is all this work connected with the Met office? If it is I wish you'd keep it there instead of messing the place up.'

'Nothing to do with the Met office, dear.' Alvin lighted his pipe thoughtfully. 'It's what you call the dream — the one which began yesterday. I'm working on the details of how to get the mastery of the weather.'

'Which has something to do with hot and cold air?'

'It has everything to do with it. Look, let me show you. Come and sit here for a moment.'

Much as one would tolerate the demands of an insistent child Nancy obeyed. She tried to look interested as Alvin's arm went about her shoulders.

'Now, dear, let me explain — May clear things up a bit for me, too. Weather is caused by enormous masses of air pressure in the atmosphere, which in themselves are governed by the motion of the earth on its axis. The high pressure areas are called anticyclones and the low pressure areas are depressions. Think of a smooth pond and call it the atmosphere. Drifting across it is an eddy, which we would — atmospherically speaking — call an anti-cyclone. Understand?'

'I think so,' Nancy agreed, but her brows were knitted. 'Where does it all lead, anyway?'

'It leads to this: Warm winds blow from the tropical regions, and cold winds from the Arctic regions. The two are always engaged in a battle with each other, and according to whichever wins a fine or a stormy area is established . . . Take a clear blue sky of even temperature. The wind shifts and cold air blows across the blue sky. There is condensation — like the steam you get in the kitchen which makes the walls wet — and condensation produces clouds, which if the condensation is particularly dense produces rain. If it is not dense you get clouds only and no rain. At times this upper cold wind descends to the ground and you get a gale. These things happen in varying degree, which brings in cold fronts, warm fronts, occlusions, and such like, about which I don't suppose you know a thing.'

'I couldn't agree more. I don't . . . ' Nancy shifted slightly. 'How long will this take? I'll have to be getting supper.'

'Supper can wait for a moment.' Alvin kissed his wife gently. 'You think I'm crazy, don't you?'

'Anything but. But you're certainly talking of things that are way beyond me. What's the point? What are you driving at?'

'One thing — control of the weather. It boils down to one thing: There's got to be a way of making hot air stay hot, and cold air stay cold. The two commingling produce all the trouble that we call weather. If, for definite periods, one consistent temperature were maintained, we'd have no upsets whatever. But that's a big thing. Very big.'

'Perhaps — too big,' Nancy suggested, but Alvin shook his head stubbornly over his pipe.

'No, I don't think so. One said that about flying, yet now aircraft span the globe as a matter of routine. Nothing is really too big if you have the wit and energy to keep on trying. There is a way round this . . . '

He broke off as the doorbell rang. Nancy detached herself from his grasp.

'That'll be David. I'll really have to have the table for supper, Alvin . . . '

He nodded absently. Moved his notes to a far corner of the room, picked up the charts; then he sat in profound meditation as his wife busied herself. He hardly remembered going to bed, so intent was he on his dream. For he had the very thing within his grasp, if only he could nail it down . . .

So for many weeks — whilst ironically the weather settled into a fine sunny spell and even allowed the picnic to be had — Alvin kept on chasing rainbows, working out mathematics, asking countless questions of his fellow Metmen without giving away too much, and generally plotting and planning, until finally he had a thick notebook full of facts. These engaged him on every free night during the autumn, and at Christmas he was still thinking about them. Then, just upon New Year as he was being dragged to a dance quite against his inclinations, he said:

'I believe I've got it, Nancy!'

'Got what?' She fixed her hair carefully before the dressing table mirror.

'The answer! The control of the climate!' Alvin sat with one immaculate shoe on and the other off, staring into space.

'You mean you're still wondering about that business?' Nancy looked at him in

16

sheer surprise. 'I thought you'd given it up long ago!'

'Only because I haven't talked about it. I've not given it up — not I! Besides, I promised David . . . I've got all the details of what could be done, but the puzzle was — how? Now I believe I've got that too . . . Look, would you listen to me for a moment?'

'I'll always listen, dear, but don't assume that I understand. Fire away. I'm paying attention.'

'Right. The puzzle up to now has been how to produce hot or cold at will and keep the atmosphere at a constant temperature. How to include such enormous air masses. *That's* been the problem. I thought of using the sun's rays, somehow magnified, for the heat — but the cold stumped me. Now I think there's another way. Heat and cold are actually molecular, you know.'

'Molecular? What's that mean?'

Alvin opened his mouth to explain, then he closed it again. He had suddenly realized — perhaps for the first time — how completely alone he really was

17

with his problem. Nancy just did not understand — not because she was stupid but because the antics of the climate were right outside her sphere of interest, except when she felt cold or got wet. On the other hand, the men at the Met office wouldn't be any help either for Alvin had not told them a thing. His theory was still too much of a theory to merit serious consideration from experts, and besides there was always the chance that he might be suspected of suffering from 'over-strain'.

'Well?' Nancy repeated. 'What's molecular?'

'It's scientific. I don't think you'd understand it dear. You see, molecules vibrate faster when they're heated, and slow down when they're cold. At absolute zero — like the void of outer space — there's no movement at all, whereas at furnace heat they dash all over the place. Never mind. It's no time to talk shop when we're going to a dance.'

And on that note Alvin closed up completely, and remained closed up to such an extent that he never mentioned his theory while at home. He nursed it himself and brooded over it in the Met office. Slowly but surely, as winter gave way to spring, he built up his idea into practical form, drawing sketches with the Met office equipment during his dinner hour. The final result, in mid-May was a drawing of a queer-looking machine which he quietly took to a firm of engineers for construction.

Early June saw his model completed. There seemed something symbolic about the fact that he took it home on an evening of drenching rain. Nancy watched curiously as, regardless of the table being laid for a meal, he put the parcel down and removed the brown paper. Then from a stiff cardboard box he brought forth a glittering object, two feet square, and looking rather like a camera except that the lens and various gadgets were located on the top instead of the side.

Nancy's wonder deepened. Young David came into the room, stared at the thing, then looked at his father's beaming face.

'What is it, dad? Something for me?'

'Don't always be thinking of yourself,

my lad,' Alvin returned cryptically. 'It's not for you, or me, or your mother. It's for everybody. Or at least it will be in the full size.'

'It isn't something to do with — the weather?' Nancy hesitated. 'You've given up that idea, haven't you? Or at any rate you've never mentioned it recently.'

'Only because I knew you wouldn't understand. Yes, this is a model of the first climatic machine, and it's demanded a good deal of hard thought and perspiration to produce it.'

Nancy did not say anything. She put her arm around David's shoulders and continued to stare at the boxlike contrivance.

'I could explain it to you, but I don't think I will,' Alvin said after a moment. 'You're no scientist, but you'll appreciate results if you see them. That being so, suppose I turned the weather around this house — a limited area, you'll understand — into sunny warmth. You'd believe that, wouldn't you?'

'Of course.' Nancy cast a glance at the disordered table. 'Do you want to test it now or after we've had tea?'

'Tea?' Alvin looked blank. 'You can talk of tea when I have this? Tea can wait. Just watch.'

Being master in his own home — or so he fondly imagined — he picked up a length of flex which trailed from the contrivance and after adjusting a transformer-pointer, pushed the plug at the end of the flex into the power socket. Then, with no more ceremony than switching on a torch, he snapped across the power button on the instrument.

Nothing happened beyond the fact that the box hummed softly in its insides. Outside, pitiless rain blasted against the windows, and sodden trees in the garden swayed mournfully before a rising gale.

'Well?' Nancy asked, after a few moments. 'What's supposed to happen? I don't see anything different.'

'You will.' Alvin was very placid. 'Give it time.'

Nancy had little choice. Besides, she was curious. It even seemed as though something ought to happen, otherwise Alvin would not have been so intent and concentrated. Though his attitude was relaxed, it was plain he was thinking hard, and listening to the hum from the box. After a moment he went to the window and peered between the thin streams of rain coursing down it.

'What exactly is supposed to happen?' Nancy asked at last, and Alvin turned sharply.

'Everything within an area of half a mile should have fine weather,' he said, shrugging. 'We're at the center of the circle, and within half a mile on every side of it, fine weather should be the answer.'

'Oh . . . I see.'

Nancy did not see at all: she was merely being polite. And she was becoming just a little frightened, too, wondering if Alvin was beginning to go 'that way' with thinking about his theory so consistently. After all, how could a shiny box with a lens on top possibly affect the weather? It just wasn't —

'It's clearing!' Alvin exclaimed suddenly, a taut, incredulous note in his voice. 'No doubt about it! See up there — a touch of blue sky!'

Nancy moved to the window. Quite unceremoniously, Alvin seized the back of her head and directed her attention upwards. She was forced then to see it — a tiny patch of blue amid the surrounding gray, and it was growing even as she watched. Wider and wider.

'That spot,' Alvin said, 'is directly over that machine of mine. The radiation from it is going vertically upwards in a straight line. Molecular activity is set up which creates a dissolution of the vapors producing the clouds and rain . . . '

Nancy stared fixedly. She had no idea what Alvin was rambling about but she was definitely interested. And with every second the blue patch extended. David came to her side and watched, too, with the fascination only a youngster could evince.

'You are sure,' Nancy asked presently, still watching the blue, 'that it isn't the blue sky that comes after a shower? This rain may only be a shower after all!'

'Shower!' Alvin exploded, scandalized. 'I'll soon show you! Get your macs on, both of you. Hurry! We're going for a walk!'

Still with the feeling that she was obeying orders of a lunatic, Nancy hurried out of the room with David beside her. She came back after a moment or two in plastic mackintosh and rain hood. Behind her loomed David in raincoat and school cap.

'Good,' Alvin said absently, and much preoccupied, he led the way out into the hall, slipped on raincoat and hat, and then opened the front door. Outside it had stopped raining even though there were sloshing puddles in the front path.

'Let's go,' Alvin said briefly. 'Half a mile. I'll show you whether it's a shower or not.'

Dutifully his wife and son followed him down the path and out into the already drying main street. Nancy looked at the sky as she went. The blueness had spread considerably now, yet in some odd way it looked circular, like an enormous oval patch overhead. At the edge of it gray cloud sailed inwards, and then disappeared when the blueness was reached.

Grimly intent on the outcome of his experiment, Alvin led the way through the suburban avenues, and after a while the sun even got through and beamed down affectionately on the trio. Then as they reached one of the farther avenues, the sunlight faded and they stepped abruptly into rain — hissing sheets of it.

'Good,' Alvin said. 'This is the limit of influence. Now look above you.'

Nancy and David did so, their eyes screwed up against the rain. Over the avenues whence they had come was blue sky, the houses gleaming in diagonal sunlight. Yet above them was writhing gray cloud, weirdly shearing off as it reached the blue. It was a classic example of 'Thus far and no farther shalt thou go!'

'Well?' Alvin asked triumphantly, rain pouring down his face. 'I've proved it was no passing shower. The rain stops, and the cloud vanishes, at the edge of influence from my machine. Are you satisfied?'

'Satisfied — and wet,' Nancy said. 'It's soaking into my shoes. For heaven's sake, let's get back.'

They took a stride forward, and the queer sunlight shafted down on them.

Behind, the rain was like a curtain.

'This is marvelous!' Alvin enthused, as they returned home through sunlit streets. 'The proofs of months of thought! You grasp why the sun is shining?' he questioned excitedly.

'I do,' David said, surprisingly, glancing above. 'It's just clear of the clouds. If it had been a bit lower there'd have been no sun.'

'Right,' Alvin approved. 'Very good, my lad. What else do you know?'

'Only that that box of yours does something to stop rain and clouds having any effect. It's a wizard idea, whatever it is.'

'It's an idea that's going to change the world, my boy,' Alvin said, speaking a great truth without realizing it. 'You and your mother have just witnessed the first practical demonstration of weather control.'

'I don't know whether to be delighted or afraid,' Nancy said, loosening the rain-smothered hood from her head. 'Aren't you sort of dabbling in things a bit too deep?'

'The eternal question.' Alvin smiled, gesturing. 'They said it to Edison, Einstein, Pasteur, Lister, Marconi — to all of them when they discovered something never heard of before. It's nothing to be afraid of, dearest. It's the masterpiece of all time.'

By this time they had come back to the house in the brilliant sunlight. Loosening his raincoat, Alvin strode through to the lounge and switched his machine off. The instant he did so there was a blinding flash of lightning outside and an almost simultaneous clap of thunder. The house shuddered to its foundations.

White-faced, Nancy hung on to the doorpost looking into the room. More curious than frightened, David stood beside her, then he pointed through the window.

'Look! It's raining again! As bad as ever.'

'Exactly,' Alvin nodded. 'The normal condition of the weather at the moment, now I've withdrawn the influence of my machine. That clap of thunder was caused by the 'pushed back' conditions abruptly coming into position again . . . rather like the forcing back of the atmosphere for a millionth of a second by a lightning flash. Or breaking the sound barrier . . . Bound to be a reaction.'

'Any — any more thunderclaps coming?' Nancy asked nervously, as Alvin unplugged his device from the power socket.

'No, no. Everything's quite normal now.'

There was a silence, rather one of incredulity, as Nancy rid herself of her outdoor things and set to work to bring order to the chaotic table. Alvin, mean-while, took a seat by the window and gave himself up to thought.

'What happens now?' Nancy asked, wide-eyed, as they sat and had tea. 'Whilst I can see you've accomplished something that's outside of the usual run of things, I can't see what benefit it is. I mean, you can't have your own private weather. If we sat in bright sun and the neighbors got drenched there'd be a terrible lot of explaining to do. If it comes to that, I daresay a lot of them are wondering what happened tonight to produce a sudden clear period followed by a clap of thunder and resumed rain.'

'Of course they're wondering,' Alvin shrugged. 'But they can't do anything about it. As for them guessing what caused it, they just haven't the brains . . . As a matter of fact, Nancy, I've come to a turning point in my career. Tomorrow I'm after bigger game than being an official at the Met office. I'm going to try to interest Big Money in the idea of weather control.'

'You mean — give up your job?' Nancy looked justifiably anxious.

'No: that wouldn't do. I've got a few days holiday due me, so I'll cash in on them. Either tomorrow or the next day I'll take a bit of time off work and get busy. This discovery's enormous — gigantic. There's no limit to what it can do. But, of course, I'll need high finance to back me.'

'Yes, of course.' And because she knew Alvin was the world's worst businessman, the anxious look did not leave her face. 'Don't let them cheat you out of anything, will you? That's a marvelous idea you've got there, and in the hands of worldly financiers you might . . . '

'I shan't,' Alvin interrupted flatly. 'I know what I'm doing, and I'll drive a tough bargain to get the backing I want.'

2

Murder

To his annoyance, Alvin had to work the following day — his holiday of four days beginning the day afterwards. So he worked to routine and pondered on what he had done the evening before. Apparently he had done enough to get the newspapers, for quite a few of the dailies posed the question — in a small column — of what had happened in a certain suburban locality of London to produce a brief weather clearance whilst everywhere around had been swamped? Even the Met Office was asked this question, and nobody could answer it. Except the quiet young man working diligently on Atlantic charts. And he only smiled to himself.

To Alvin, with so much locked up inside him, the day at the Met office seemed interminable. When at last it came to an end he made for home as quickly as possible, and spent the evening collecting all notes and data regarding his weather machine for presentation to the right party on the morrow.

'Whom are you going to approach?' Nancy questioned.

'I'm not sure yet. There are three likely financiers who might be interested — Nicholas Sutherland, Sir Robert Bentley or Marcus Denham. They are all pretty broad-minded in their approach to something new, and I do know that Marcus Denham is something of a scientist as well . . . Have to see.'

Of the three prospective financiers, Alvin chose Nicholas Sutherland first when he started off next day, his 'weather box' inside a big suitcase. As usual it was raining, that drizzly sort of stuff that soaks through and through. Protected by his small car, Alvin was, for once, not complaining at the weather. It was just what he needed for a demonstration.

Toward 10.30 he reached the Sutherland Oil Corporation's headquarters — a vast edifice of granite and chromium signs in the heart of the city. The very sight of it, and the wealth and power it represented, stalled Alvin for a moment. Then he took a hold of himself again, drove into the building car park, and thence proceeded into the main hallway of the edifice. Almost immediately a braided commissionaire loomed and inquired briefly of his business.

'Mr. Sutherland in person,' Alvin explained cheerfully. 'I must have an interview with him.'

'You have an appointment?'

'Well, no. My name's Alvin Brook, and my concern is oil. I represent a Texan firm . . . I'm sure Mr. Sutherland will see me.'

The commissionaire looked as though he doubted it, but nevertheless he departed majestically to regions unknown and left Alvin with his fingers crossed . . . Evidently to some purpose, for after a while the commissionaire came back, gravely polite.

'Mr. Sutherland has a few moments; sir, if you will step this way.'

Alvin obeyed. He was conducted through opulent corridors, into fast

33

elevators, through softly lighted ante-rooms, and at last into the office of Nicholas Sutherland himself, a small, birdlike man with a face of childish smoothness and a manner of genial conciseness.

'Mr. Sutherland,' Alvin smiled, shaking hands. 'Forgive me taking up your time.'

'Not at all — glad to meet anybody connected with oil. Now, Mr — er — Brook, what did you wish to see me about?'

'Well, it's nothing to do with oil,' Alvin said frankly. 'That was an excuse to get into your presence. I knew you'd probably be suddenly busy if I explained my real purpose.'

'Ingenuity is always to be commended, Mr. Brook. What *is* your real purpose?'

'Control of the weather.'

Sutherland was too old a hand to give a start. Instead he took a deep drag at his cigarette and then smiled like a cherub.

'The weather, eh? Well, that's original, anyhow — even if I don't see any connection between it and oil.'

'You, sir, are a financier,' Alvin hurried

on. 'I might even say you're one of the richest men in the country. I also know you have backed many projects in your time. I'm looking for a backer now. Complete control of the climate, anywhere in the world, at the touch of a button.'

'How very intriguing. I have never before been asked to gamble on the weather. At least you are an original young man, Mr. Brook.'

'I don't expect you to believe anything without proof. Let me show you. For instance, it's raining outside.'

'Of that I'm aware.'

'In 10 minutes I can give you fine weather for half a mile around in a circle, this building being the center.'

Sutherland seemed about to say something when the telephone buzzed. He picked it up, kept his gray eyes on Alvin, and fired off a lot of meaningless comments. Finally he put the phone down and rose to his feet. The smile of a cherub was back again.

'I am so sorry, Mr. Brook, but my presence is requested elsewhere in the building at the moment. Some other time, eh? You've quite intrigued me. Really!'

'Any time,' Alvin said, eagerly. 'How about tomorrow?'

'Mmm — uncertain.' Sutherland was moving vaguely toward the door. 'How about leaving your address, then I can fix a date. I'm a very busy man, as, of course, you realize.'

Alvin fumbled in his pocket and pulled out his wallet. From it he extracted a card and handed it over.

'There you are, Mr. Sutherland. I'm entirely at your disposal.'

'Splendid — splendid.' Sutherland shook hands, beamed, and opened the door. Alvin picked up his equipment and went out into the corridor knowing perfectly well that he had seen the last of Nicholas Sutherland. Probably the telephone gag was rigged anyway to get him away from unwanted callers.

'All right,' Alvin muttered fiercely as he stepped out into the clinging drizzle. 'All right! There are others, thank goodness, and some day Mr. Bigshot Sutherland, you'll realize what you've missed.'

Disappointed, but by no means despondent, Alvin set off again — and in half an hour he was invading the headquarters of Sir Robert Bentley.

Here he drew a complete blank. The great man was away, out of the country. Just nothing could be done. Muttering to himself, Alvin departed, had a quick lunch, and then invaded the third member on his list — Marcus Denham.

Here he drew lucky. Marcus Denham granted an interview, and toward 2.30 Alvin was shown into his office.

Denham, immaculate and hefty, rose from his desk and came across the room as Alvin entered. He shook hands with a great warm paw and beamed from a fleshy, unusually florid face.

'Glad to know you, Mr. Brook,' he greeted. 'Something about engineering, didn't you say?'

'Well, yes,' Alvin admitted, as he was waved to a chair. 'But it's not entirely true. My basic idea is engineering, in which your firm is interested, but I've a deeper purpose.'

'All right, let's have it.' Denham sat down again and pushed over a box of cigars. He lighted Alvin's cigar and looked at him with curiously small blue eyes over the fragrant smoke.

'It's about the weather,' Alvin said, as calmly as he could.

'Oh? What about it?'

'In this box here,' Alvin said, pointing to it on the carpet, 'I have the means to control it, in model form, that is . . . As you'll agree, that is a form of engineering.'

'And science,' Denham added, speculative thought masking his blue eyes. 'Keep right on talking. Sounds good.'

Definitely encouraged, Alvin continued: 'I have the means of control, and I can demonstrate right at this moment. I believe you are something of a scientist yourself?'

'I have degrees for it,' Denham admitted. 'You must be one yourself to have thought of such a thing.'

'Not exactly. I'm a Met man, with a definite grievance against the English climate. It occurred to me how many

38

things could benefit from control of the weather — not only in England, but anywhere in the world — '

'No doubt of that, but how do you do it? That's the part I'm interested in.'

'I'll explain, without giving away too much.' Alvin smiled. 'I work on the basic premise, proven correct, that any form of weather upset is created by the interchange of hot and cold air currents. They're always at war with each other. Eliminate one, and disturbance is reduced to zero. If you have abundant rain, as we have, it's caused by condensation, which is the fusion of heat and cold, producing clouds that finally reach dew point and start to drop rain. On the other hand if we have a crippling cold spell we can break it down by a warm air front. The clouds which would form normally can be broken up by just the right amount of heat or cold — enough to balance, if you understand.'

'Oh, I do!' Denham's graying head nodded emphatically. 'Go on, by all means. How do you produce your heat or cold? Tall order, isn't it?'

'It was at first, but I got the better of it. I reduce it to a common matter of molecular vibration, which is of course the main cause of what we know as heat and cold. The faster the vibration of the molecules the greater the heat, and vice versa.'

'That's true enough, but how do you produce the molecular vibration?'

'Simple enough.' Alvin again indicated his model. 'In this instrument there is an electrical set up. It emits a beam through this lens on the top. Naturally, the beam fans out as it goes, until when it reaches the higher atmosphere it is including an area of about a mile — that is, half a mile on every side from the center. Right?'

'But what's the nature of the beam?'

'Purely vibration. Many things are done by vibration these days, but I think this is the first time that vibration, as such, has been applied directly to the molecules of the atmosphere . . . Picture this: There are clouds at about 2,000 feet, as at present. Into them plunges the vibratory beam. The molecules of the cloud, widely spaced because it is in gaseous form, either vibrate more rapidly or move less slowly, according to the vibration used. If less vibration the clouds thicken: if more is used they start to thin, finally vanishing when their temperature is the same as the prevailing temperature around them. It is only the variance in temperature which causes clouds in the first place.'

'By which means you could also cause clouds to form in an otherwise clear sky?'

'Exactly. Given the temperature of the air at a certain point over the Earth, one emits a vibratory beam calculated to get the molecules of the air vibrating at a different rate from the rest of the air. The difference would be construed as difference in temperature. That area being hotter, or colder, than the immediate surroundings, cloud would form. If continued far enough dew point would be reached and rain would follow.'

'Very, very interesting.' Marcus Denham was so absorbed the ash on his cigar was still unbroken.

'Naturally, I speak only of the model,' Alvin resumed, after a moment. 'It is sufficient to demonstrate with. What I really have in mind is a series of climatic machines at different parts of the world, together with a small air force employed solely for the purpose of testing the temperature of the atmosphere. That way the various machines could be geared to give out just the right amount of vibration to keep the atmosphere at one temperature, and any incoming air currents would automatically be converted to the equalizing temperature, preventing cloud formation . . . That would produce a fine weather anticyclone for as long as it was needed. If rain were required, 'different temperature' areas could be created over a stagnant area, and a depression and storm produced at will.'

Denham got to his feet and the ash sprayed down his ample waistcoat. Musing to himself he went across to the window and gazed for a moment at the steadily descending drizzle.

'I don't think you realize,' he said slowly, without turning, 'what a tremendous visionary you are, Mr. Brook. Why, the ramifications of this idea are endless.'

'It certainly has possibilities,' Alvin

admitted modestly.

'Possibilities!' Denham swung round. 'Why, dammit man, the human race has been searching after something like this ever since the caveman days. Millions are lost every year through the wild caprices of the weather. In peace and in war it is the governing force. With it mastered almost anything — anything — is possible.'

Alvin nodded. For some reason he did not quite like the look in Denham's small blue eyes. There was a kind of avaricious glitter.

'Show me!' Denham ordered abruptly. 'You say you can do a small demonstration on the spot — All right, let's see what you can do with a foul day like this.'

Alvin nodded and quietly went to work, watched all the time by the interested magnate. The model was plugged into a power socket, switched on, and then came the period of waiting. Denham drew hard on his cigar as he gazed out of the window, then at length he nearly snatched the weed out of his mouth as he gazed upwards.

'By all the saints, I do believe you're right!' he exclaimed. 'There's blue sky coming into view.'

'Of course,' Alvin said, and waited.

Like a man watching a miracle, Denham remained by the window, his smoldering cigar in his fingers. Then at last sunlight shafted down and set the raindrops on the glass scintillating with all the colors of the spectrum.

'It's as easy as that,' Alvin said, coming to the financier's side. 'Fine day — wet day — at the touch of a button . . . But, of course, to put it on a proper basis it needs money — oceans of it, and I just haven't got it.'

'But you've got ideas, man! Marvelous ideas! And the world is always willing to pay for them. In this case, I'm the one who'll pay for them. We're going to talk business, Mr. Brook. Switch off the fine weather and let's get down to facts.'

Alvin touched the button on his machine. There was a lapse of a few seconds and then the customary flash of lightning and reverberating thunder.

'What's that?' Denham asked, frowning,

44

as the drizzle returned.

'Just the normal air pressure resuming its position. Nothing to be alarmed about.'

'I'm not alarmed: I'm just wondering about something. Suppose you had all the world under climatic control and then suddenly stopped all of it with a master switch. What would happen?'

Alvin reflected. 'I don't really know: I've never pondered on it, simply because I don't suppose any responsible scientist, in charge of weather machines, would do such an idiotic thing . . . I imagine the result of simultaneous stoppage the world over would be disastrous. All the natural air currents would suddenly swing into being, impelled as ever by the revolution of the Earth.'

'Mmm, wants thinking about,' Denham mused, sitting at the desk. 'However, to more practical matters . . . I suppose you've got blueprints and specifications of this invention? Something for engineers to work on?'

'Decidedly. They're in my car. I didn't bring them until I felt I was on safe ground. There are stacks of them.'

Denham grinned. 'Wise man. All right, I'll put my cards on the table. You've shown me something practical, and I'm scientist enough to know that what you've said is quite logical. To that you have added your demonstration. I'm willing to back you to the hilt on one condition.'

'And what's that?'

'That you relinquish all rights whatever to the invention and let me handle it — or at any rate my company. Inventions are often handled under license, but that isn't my way. I'm an all or nothing man.'

'Which virtually divests me of all credit for the invention?'

'The compensation is measured in money, Mr. Brook. I'll pay you fifteen million to forget that you ever invented weather control.'

Alvin was silent but his thoughts were hurrying. Denham waited, picked a cigar out of the silver box, and sniffed at it.

'Bearing everything in mind,' Alvin said at length, 'I'd say it's worth twenty million of anybody's money. The oil companies paid that clear of tax to a man who invented a perfect substitute for petrol, and this is even bigger than that. On the other hand, I realize that you'll have heavy expense in the building of machines the world over — so split the difference and say seventeen and a half million.'

'Seventeen million, five hundred thousand pounds,' Denham reflected, lighting his cigar. 'Let me think about that. Nip down to your car and get your blueprints and specifications whilst I ponder. I don't suppose you feel like trusting anyone else to get them.'

'Hardly,' Alvin said, and departed. He was beginning to feel dizzy with circumstances. £17,500,000! If it came off, he'd be a multi-millionaire. Fixed for life . . . In less than no time he was back in Denham's office with his briefcase in his hand.

'I am prepared to accept your offer,' the tycoon said slowly, giving the impression he had weighed everything beforehand. 'Seventeen million and five hundred thousand it is. For that you agree to waive everything and hand over to me.'

'Of course,' Alvin assented, hoping he looked calm. 'All the facts are here in my briefcase — '

'No doubt, but before that, answer me one or two questions. First, does anybody else know the details of this invention?'

Alvin shook his head.

'Have you a wife and family? If so, how much do they know?'

'I have a wife and a young son. My wife doesn't have the least idea of what I'm driving at — and, of course, my son hasn't, at his age.'

'Good. And there's nobody else?'

'Nobody.' Alvin frowned slightly. 'Does it matter, anyway?'

'Of course it does. I am buying the exclusive right to your discovery, so naturally I want to know if anybody else has . . . nibbled.' Denham grinned suddenly. 'All right, I'm satisfied. Now to business. Naturally I cannot part with that kind of money without being absolutely sure of what I'm doing. I want time to look over the details of your design and specifications. I am prepared to give you a signed agreement as a receipt. And, for giving me an exclusive option to consider it, a post-dated check for £10,000 payable in three days — which is approximately the time it will take me to sort everything out. Are you agreeable?'

Alvin sniffed around mentally for snags, but failed to detect any. He nodded slowly.

'All right, it's a deal, but on my side I want a proviso that you will have your decision ready in three days. I don't want indefinite delays. I want action.'

'You'll get it,' Denham promised, and snapped the button on the intercom. 'Miss Carlyle? Come here a moment and bring your notebook. I want an agreement drafted . . . '

★   ★   ★

Alvin left the Denham office with an agreement duly signed and a check for £10,000 payable in three days' time. He felt entirely satisfied with himself and pleased with his business acumen. Even the perpetual drizzle could not damp his spirits, and once he got home Nancy listened interestedly to all he had to say. At first her excited joy knew no bounds, then something of her feminine instinct started to slow down her exultation.

'And Denham now has everything to study? The model included?' she asked, when Alvin stopped talking.

'Certainly. I just said so.'

'Mmm . . . ' Nancy looked thoughtful. Young David went on eating, not particularly interested in developments, anyway.

'What's the matter?' Alvin asked presently; and Nancy gave a start.

'Oh, nothing really. I just don't like the thought of all your notes and specifications being in Denham's hands. And the model, too, if it comes to that. All you've got is £10,000, and an agreement. You can't even cash the check for three days.'

'Well, what's wrong with that? I can't expect Denham to pay up without knowing what he's getting. My demonstration wasn't enough in itself: he wants to know what makes things tick. So would I in his position. I'll be all right, don't you worry.'

And, manlike, with his head definitely in and above the clouds, Alvin did not worry any further. Drizzle or otherwise, he decided to start enjoying his holiday, with the result that Nancy and David found themselves whirled through the soggy countryside for an evening's run, ending up at a remote motel for supper. Nancy could have enjoyed it thoroughly if only she had not had a nagging doubt at the back of her mind.

Then, back home again through the clearing weather, and to bed at half-past eleven. Alvin slept soundly, at peace with the world — but not Nancy. That worry was still eating at her mind, and for the life of her she could not think why. After all, everything was in order, and there was no reason to suppose that Denham was a crook. In vain Nancy tried to convince herself that not all financiers are dishonest, but she could not rid herself of the realization that Alvin was no business-man, and nobody would be quicker to detect that than the razor-sharp Marcus Denham.

Though Nancy said nothing to Alvin at

51

breakfast next morning concerning her doubts, her very quietness was something that puzzled Alvin quite a lot. With £17,500,000 in the offing, he just could not understand what had occasioned an attack of the doldrums, and he had no chance to inquire for, just as breakfast was starting, the telephone rang.

'Yes? Alvin Brook speaking — '

'Oh, hello, Mr. Brook!' It was the unmistakable voice of Marcus Denham, full of lusty good humor. 'Glad I caught you before you got out for the day — Look, I had an unexpected opportunity to examine those plans and specifications of yours.'

'Good. And what do you think of them?'

'They're everything you claim, and I'm not relying on my own judgment when I say that, either. I had my scientific staff check as well . . . To cut it short, Mr. Brook, I'm entirely satisfied. Can you be at my office this morning to complete our business?'

Alvin smiled into the mouthpiece. 'I'll be there. What time shall it be?'

'Say around 10. I'm phoning from home, of course.' There was a brief pause, then: 'Tell you a better idea. I have to pass your avenue on the way to town: I'll have the car call for you. You'll get in easier with me by your side, eh?'

'Into the Denham building, you mean?' Alvin gave a laugh. 'Yes, it's always a good idea to ride with the boss.'

'Right. I'll pick you up — 9.30 prompt. Be punctual.'

'For seventeen million plus, what do you think?' Alvin chuckled, and then he rang off. He became aware of Nancy watching him from the lounge door.

'Marcus Denham, I presume?' she asked.

'Yes my love — and we're in the money!' Alvin strode forward and swept her up into his arms. 'Denham has checked the blueprints and specifications and that seventeen and a half million is ours!'

For the moment Nancy forgot all her anxieties and kissed her husband ardently as he held her, then slowly he lowered her to her feet.

'He's coming at 9.30 to pick me up, he said. 'I'd better give myself an extra polish up — '

'Pick you up?' Nancy repeated, as he

dived for the stairs. 'Why can't you go yourself? You know the way, don't you?'

'He's passing the door in his car. I'll have no difficulty if I'm with him. You've no idea what a job it is trying to contact him in that wilderness he controls.'

Alvin was on his way, singing in a lusty baritone as he headed for the bathroom. Nancy stood where she was, a slight frown marring her pretty face; then as David called for some trifling thing or other she went on her way into the lounge.

And, right on time, Marcus Denham arrived, in the biggest car ever seen in Alvin's quiet little avenue. The financier did not come into the house: he merely instructed his chauffeur to blow the horn, which was sufficient to bring the ready-and-waiting Alvin into view, his wife beside him. Only then did Denham lower the window of the car and peer outside, his florid face wreathed in somehow unconvincing smiles.

'Ready, Mr. Brook?' he inquired.

'Ready — and willing.' Alvin came down the pathway, holding on to his wife's arm. 'Meet my wife, Mr. Denham. Nancy, this is Mr. Denham himself. Probably your one and only chance to see one of the biggest financiers in the country at close quarters.'

Nancy smiled rather uncomfortably as a gray-suited arm reached through the car window and an enormous hand grasped hers.

'So you're Mr. Brook's little lady? Delighted! Take good care of him, Mrs. Brook. With ideas like he can turn out he ought to be kept in cotton wool.'

Nancy laughed, hardly knowing what she ought to say. Denham's personality somehow overpowered her. She turned to Alvin and kissed him as he stood with his hand on the car door.

'By-by, dearest — for the moment.'

Denham cleared his throat and waited, his broad smile never relaxing. Then at last Alvin was finished with his farewell. He climbed into the car and sank down in the soft cushions — but he still waved vigorously through the car's rear window as it glided out of the avenue into the main road.

'Evidently you have quite an affection for your wife, Mr. Brook,' Denham commented, as the journey into town began.

'Certainly I have: she's all in all to me. Natural, isn't it?'

'I wouldn't really know.' Denham grinned. 'Personally, I find my own wife a bit of a damned nuisance. Truth to tell, most women are. Too nosey. Know too much.'

Alvin stared for a moment, half prompted to take up a stand for the opposite sex, then remembering his £17,500,000 he decided it might be better to keep quiet.

'You say your wife doesn't understand anything about this invention of yours?' Denham asked presently, as they sped into the heart of the city.

'Nothing at all. She isn't scientific.'

'But surely she's got some idea of what you're doing? She must know, I take it, that you can control the weather?'

'Oh, yes, she knows. But she doesn't know how I do it — and I don't think she cares very much either, just so long as I do it.'

Denham became silent, obviously following a line of thought. Vaguely, Alvin wondered what it was. Why Denham should be interested in Nancy's reactions was a complete mystery to him. Perhaps, if he had been a keener man in judging character, suspicion might have been born. But it was not. He merely assumed that Marcus Denham was making small talk.

Denham entered his office at 9.45, with Alvin beside him. What happened in the office only those two men knew. The odd thing was that Alvin never came out. He vanished into thin air, and Denham went on with his work, dealing with various members of his staff as the day progressed, and not one of them saw any trace of Alvin Brook.

It was toward 2.30 in the afternoon when Denham's phone rang on the main wire. He lifted it, writing on his scratch pad at the same time.

'Yes? Denham speaking . . . '

'Hello, Mr. Denham. This is Nancy Brook speaking — Alvin's wife.'

'Oh, yes! How are you?' Denham

reached out to a switch and pushed it down. That meant the line was exclusive between himself and Nancy Brook.

'I'm getting a bit worried, Mr. Denham. Alvin hasn't come home yet, and naturally with so much at stake I'm a bit excited — maybe unduly so. Is he still with you?'

'As a matter of fact, he is. We were just deciding to have a small celebration, and it occurred to me that there's no reason why you shouldn't be in it, too — as Alvin's wife.'

'I'd love to,' came Nancy's eager voice.

'Good. Then come over here as soon as you can. I'll tell the commissionaire you're coming, so you'll have no difficulty when you arrive. You can do that?'

'Certainly I can. I'll tell my sister to have an eye to David, then I'll be along.'

'Your sister?' Denham repeated, vaguely.

'Yes. She only lives a few doors away. She looks after David when I have to go out. David's our son, you know.'

'Of course, of course. How silly of me. All right, Mrs. Brook, come as soon as you can.'

Denham put the telephone back on its

cradle and reflected for a moment, then he snapped the intercom button.

'Yes, Mr. Denham?' came the voice of the commissionaire in the entrance hall.

'In a short while a Mrs. Brook will be coming, George. She's a young, rather pretty woman, Show her straight up to my office.'

'Very good, Mr. Denham.'

Denham switched off and lighted a cigar slowly. Then he got to his feet and looked musingly through the window.

'A risk, I know,' he muttered, 'but it's as near watertight as can be. It's worth a chance to grab something like this. Control of the weather! What can I not do with that . . . ?'

He looked at the sunny sky and then down into the city. He turned and surveyed the smooth, glossy walls of his office with hardly a hair-thin crack to show where the panels were fitted. Finally he smiled broadly to himself and went back to his desk. He remained at it until Nancy was shown in to him half an hour later.

'Ah, Mrs. Brook, do come in.' Denham

got to his feet and grasped her right hand in both of his. 'So nice to see you again. Have a seat.'

Nancy sat down slowly: She knew, she could feel, that there was something wrong somewhere.

'Er — where's Alvin?' she asked presently. 'I rather thought he would have been here.'

'Alvin? Yes, he's here.' Denham's smile faded as he stood with his hands behind him, a hard look creeping into his florid face. 'He'll always be here, in fact.'

'Always?' A startled look came into Nancy's eyes. 'How do you mean? *What* do you mean? You said — '

'I know what I said, and I meant it. He'll always be here.'

'But that's absurd! You can't keep him prisoner . . . '

'I'm not doing. He'll always be here because he can't help himself . . . Let me tell you something, Mrs. Brook. Your husband discovered one of the most powerful weapons in the world, and for that there has to be a price.'

'Weapon? Price?' Nancy stared fixedly

at the small blue eyes relentlessly piercing her. 'I don't understand. Alvin didn't invent a weapon — only control of the weather. It's an idea that can bring great benefits to everybody.'

'Admitted — particularly to those who have the secret. And Alvin Brook is not the kind of man to have a secret like that. It's far too big . . . He handed it to me, and now it's mine.'

'For £17,500,000 — yes. That was the arrangement.'

Denham took a turn round the office. Nancy's frightened eyes followed his every move, her heart thudding painfully.

'Mrs. Brook, I will be frank.' Denham said at last. 'I never had any intention of paying £17,500,000 for your husband's idea, even though my scientists found that it was a perfectly logical engineering conception. No, I don't ever pay sums like that when there is an easier way. Enormous concerns are built up on other things besides money.'

'For — for instance?' Nancy asked, hardly realizing what she was saying.

'There arises at times the necessity for

elimination, Mrs. Brook. When a person knows a great deal, and is a fool in his general outlook, it is obvious that it is far simpler to eliminate him than to pay him a big sum of money. With a keen man such an attempt would be difficult, if not at all possible. With a fool it is easy. Unhappily,' Denham sighed, 'your husband was a fool.'

'Was?' Nancy repeated. Then she sprang from her chair. 'Did you say was? What have you done with him? From the very start I felt that there was something wrong! Where is he?'

Denham reflected for a moment, his eyes on Nancy's distraught face. Then he shrugged to himself and pressed a button. Instantly one of the panels on the wall shot back, revealing a black space beyond.

'He's in there,' Denham said, indicating the aperture. 'Look for yourself . . . '

Hardly daring to think what she was going to see, yet drawn by fascination to the opening, Nancy moved forward. The nearer she came to the big aperture the stronger became a warm wind blowing about her. It disturbed her hair, set her skirt fluttering. There was a decidedly strong draught blowing from somewhere below.

'Where — ?' she began, turning — and she was just in time to see Denham's great hands thrusting toward her. They struck her violently in the chest, toppling her backwards. Helplessly, she slipped over the edge of the aperture and went down into blackness, a gasping scream wrenched from her lips.

Perspiration wet on his face, Denham turned back to his desk and snapped the panel switch. The panel closed and became an undetectable part of the wall. Alvin Brook had gone, so had his wife into the wide space between the party walls of Denham's office and the general office.

Denham's office on the topmost floor was 1,000 feet above the foundations of the edifice.

3

Denham plans

Half an hour after Nancy Brook had plunged into the 1,000-foot shaft between the party walls, a small, austere man with eyes as pale and keen as a snake's came into Denham's office. He moved with a preciseness that gave a hint as to his calling — Big time lawyer Robert Carlow, and as about as crooked a legal man as ever practiced behind a brass plate.

'Well, what this time?' Carlow asked, sitting at the desk with easy familiarity. 'Sounded pretty urgent, to judge from your voice on the phone.'

'It is.' Denham was quite composed as he pushed across the cigar box. 'I've just paid a very high price for a very valuable secret.'

'Why should you want me for that?' Carlow lighted a cigar and watched the smoke curl upwards. 'What price have you paid?'

'Murder,' Denham explained simply; and that made the lawyer start ever so slightly.

'Murder! Dammit man, what sort of lawyer do you think I am? I can't get you out of a murder spot unless its exceptionally well covered with an airtight alibi, and even then I'd have to work hard. You're high profile, and not frightfully popular, you know.'

'Shut up a minute whilst I explain. I've killed a man and his wife because they were a source of danger. Had they lived I would have had seventeen and a half million to find. There lives are not that valuable — not to me, anyhow. The two I've murdered are Alvin Brook, an obscure meteorologist, and his wife. Where their bodies are I alone know, but I can guarantee they'll never be found.'

'Then what are you worrying about? No bodies — no murder charge. That's obvious.'

'There are other considerations. For

one thing there's a son — twelve years of age. He'll start wondering about things, and though he's not at an age to reason things out very clearly he'll be able to tell the police, when they start looking into things, that his father and mother were last seen coming to my office. That will shift the focus straight to me.'

'Well?'

'I shan't answer anything: I'll refer the police to you. You know the facts now. Use your imagination for the rest.'

Carlow darted a glance from his snaky eyes. 'Always expecting miracles, aren't you? Presumably the last place this man and his wife were seen is here?'

'Yes. They were seen to come here, but not to leave. I shall say they *did* leave, so what happened after that is none of my business.'

'It may not be so easy as you think, Denham.'

Denham glared. 'It had better be! That's what I pay you for, to get me out of scrapes. Spare no expense to keep me clear.'

'Might I ask what prompted you to

murder? It must have been something exceptionally attractive.'

'It was. Nothing less than control of the climate — the perfect surefire way of doing it, given enough capital. And I certainly have that. Maybe your hide-bound legal brain can't realize it, but the man who controls the weather dictates his own terms.'

'With you controlling it I can well believe it,' Carlow murmured, getting to his feet. 'And you had to commit murder to get the secret? Well, I suppose you know your own business best, and, of course, I'll do what I can to protect you from — '

'Don't just do what you can!' Denham snapped. 'Get the police off my track at the earliest moment!'

'I'll try. The police have a habit — and also the right — of snooping incessantly when bodies disappear. As long as those bodies are never found you're compara-tively safe. The only other snag might be if anybody else knows of this weather secret.'

'Nobody that matters. Brook's wife was

the only one, and she certainly can't talk now. Brook didn't mention his discovery to anybody else. I made certain on that point.'

'And the young son?'

'At his age he's not worth considering.'

'Children soon grow up. Any normal boy losing his father and mother mysteriously might make things awkward as he grows older.'

Denham shrugged. 'There are always ways and means. I'll have a watch kept over him.'

Carlow knocked his cigar ash into the tray. 'All right, let me handle things. The man and wife came in here but did not leave and therefore — ' Carlow stopped, musing. 'Anything else I should know? Any incriminating documents, agreements, checks . . . ?'

'Nothing. There was an agreement, which has vanished along with Brook himself. An un-cashed check for £10,000 has gone the same way . . . There may be odds and ends that I've missed, but we'll fiddle round them. There's no legal proof that weather control was Brook's in the first place. It's mine now, and that's all that counts.'

'I hope you'll think it was worth it . . . I should feel happier if the son had been taken care of.'

'He may be, later.' Denham reflected through an interval. 'It all depends. And don't get the wrong idea, Carlow. I don't snuff out lives for the fun of it. In this case it had to be done.'

'Apparently so — and somewhat clumsily too, if I may say so. If those bodies are ever found between the walls — '

'A thousand feet down in the foundations, and me owning the building? No subterranean or tunnel work will ever be done without my permission, and that's the only way those bodies could be found. It was a better method than you think, even if it was melodramatic. How else would you have suggested I got rid of them?'

'I don't know: I haven't a mind like yours.' Carlow grinned unpleasantly and picked up his hat from the desk. 'All right, I know the situation, and I'll do my best to protect you . . . I managed it in the case of Barlow, Turner, and Latham — who vanished without trace — so I suppose I can do it with the Brooks.'

With that the lawyer departed. Denham looked grimly at the closed door for a moment, then he resumed his seat at the desk. After a moment he switched on the intercom.

'Yes, Mr. Denham?'

'Send Mr. Richards in to me right away.'

Denham switched off and waited, chewing his cigar. Then Richards, chief scientist of the Denham organization, came in — a tall, keen, entirely resourceful individual.

'I'm not going to waste time,' Denham said, indicating a chair. 'I want you to work out in detail what has to be done to establish a chain of weather stations round the globe. I want to know how much machinery you'll need, how much labor, and how long it will take. I've got the go-ahead now, and everything is up to me.'

'It's going to cost tens of millions,'

Richards said. 'I can tell you that before I even work out the details. And how about the various permits from different governments?'

'To erect weather stations in their countries, you mean? Leave that to me. I'll fix it somehow.'

'Very well. I've got the various charts and specifications in my office and I'll get to work immediately.' The scientist reflected for a moment. 'Might I ask a question, sir?'

'Well?'

'What do you get out of this weather-control idea? Surely something more than a sunny day for the millions you'll have to spend. Where does the profit come in?'

'I'm surprised that isn't obvious,' Denham grinned. 'I intend to put myself in a position where every country on earth will have to pay me certain dues in order to have the weather they desire. Remember the days of the gangsters, when the ordinary public had to pay certain sums for 'protection'? Well, this is similar, but on a world-wide scale, and nobody will realize how much of a gangster technique really exists until it's too late.'

'Suppose one country doesn't agree to your terms? What's to stop them pulling down the weather machine which is in their particular country?'

'Nothing,' Denham admitted, 'but the consequences to them might be disastrous. A cyclone perhaps, a deluge. The weather is an almighty powerful weapon when you have the mastery of it. I don't think any man has possessed such unlimited power as I am going to get. From the first moment I saw the possibilities.'

The scientist shrugged. He could see clearly enough where everything was leading, but if he wanted to keep his well-paid job it was not politic to make comment. Instead he got to his feet.

'That be all then, sir? Shall I work out those estimates you want?'

'Yes — as quickly as you can, and I hope I don't have to remind you that everything is in the strictest confidence.'

Richards nodded and went out. Smiling to himself, Denham drew at his cigar and gazed through the window. The endless possibilities of the idea Alvin Brook had developed into a practicality were only just commencing to dawn upon him . . .

★   ★   ★

Naturally, as scientist Richards worked steadily on the estimates for the weather stations, there was considerable trouble brewing over the disappearance of Alvin Brook and his wife. First, her sister reported to the police that she had not returned home; and on the other hand, after his short holiday was up, the Met office wanted to know what had become of Alvin Brook.

From the ordinary local police, the matter spread to Scotland Yard, and to one of the best inspectors in the force. Inevitably the last movements of Alvin Brook and his wife were traced back to Marcus Denham, and the tycoon had several unpleasant hours answering the cross-questions of the inspector. Sometimes lawyer Carlow was present — sometimes not. In the end, just as Denham had expected, the police came up against a brick wall. On the one hand they could not make an arrest on a charge of murder because no bodies had been discovered; nor could they implicate Denham in the disappearance because nobody had ever seen Alvin Brook or his wife leave the Denham building. The inspector had many suspicions, but the limits of the law tied his hands. After a fortnight of investigation, the inspector was compelled to put the business in the 'Cases Uncompleted' file and wait for the one chance that might give him the opportunity to start ferreting again.

So, in the various media the 'disappearance' of Alvin Brook and his wife, and the possible connection of tycoon Marcus Denham in relation thereto, began to have less weight — and finally went out of fashion altogether. Only then did Marcus Denham breathe again and start to lay his plans on the estimates which scientist Richards had submitted.

The first move was a general publicity campaign, in radio, newspapers and television. Not a very difficult task since

Denham himself owned all three means of advertising — or at least had a lion's share in them. Accordingly the theme of 'Do you want weather to order?' was plugged extensively and relentlessly for several weeks, and the general public was invited to submit suggestions to the radio, television or newspaper authority concerned . . . From out of this there came the general report that the public would welcome weather ready-made, on which they could always rely. This, of course, applied to England and the West European countries, always the most maligned when it came to climatic vagary.

Two people were particularly concerned over this weather-control 'plug' — two people among the millions who merely regarded it as a publicity stunt. The two people were Dora Lester, sister of Nancy Brook, who had now adopted young David and was bringing him up with her own family — and the other person was Nicholas Sutherland, the oil magnate. Dora Lester, for her part, knew that weather control had been Alvin's invention — Nancy had hinted as much

— and, of course, Sutherland knew he had turned down such a suggestion as impractical. Both of them also knew that Alvin and his wife had disappeared. How then had Marcus Denham got hold of the idea of weather control?

For Dora Lester there was merely the infuriating realization that she could do nothing about it. Since the law could not prove anything, what chance did she stand? Sutherland, however, was a man of power and influence, and he hated Marcus Denham like poison. Further, he was annoyed with himself that he had slipped up in not having anything to do with Brook's invention. Somehow Denham had got hold of it, and there was a breath of criminal work behind the scenes, too. Sutherland was prepared to wait and start moving when the time came.

Meanwhile, Denham forged ahead, quite satisfied that nobody of importance knew that the idea of weather control was not his own. If he had known that Nicholas Sutherland had had first refusal he would probably have not been so complacent. The only person he felt he had any need to fear was David Brook, and he would not constitute a threat until he was a good deal older. By that time something could be done . . .

Having satisfied himself that the public in general took kindly to the idea of weather control, Denham moved into the second phase of his plan. He contacted the various governments whose countries would be needed in the general climatic plan, and flew to interview these VIPs. His tremendous financial influence, his scientific knowledge, and his general charm of manner — when he chose to use it — secured for him all the rights he desired. After three months of intensive journeying from Arctic to Tropics he returned to Britain a much satisfied man. Then, a brief pause whilst he assembled his array of facts, and afterwards he called together a special meeting of certain experts, in the scientific and engineering fields, headed by Richards. Before them he laid the facts.

'Gentlemen,' he said, at the head of the long, polished table, 'we are entering upon an era unheard of in the history of the world, and I seek your approval for the founding of a weather corporation . . . All of you will know, from our various radio, television and newspaper concerns that I have been hammering the idea of weather control to the general public for some time past. Now it has come to the point where, waiting only for your blessing, it has become an established fact.'

The men nodded among themselves but said nothing. Sensing he had captured their interest, Denham proceeded:

'As Mr. Richards here will verify, the establishment of weather control relies upon many weather machines, all working in perfect union. Between them they have to maintain a balance in the general atmospheric conditions, otherwise the outcome would be disastrous. Let one machine get ahead or behind the others in its functions and the various 'natural' air pressures, as we will call them, would come crowding in with unpredictable results. That has all been worked out in the master blueprint. Our main concern is the profit we shall make with these stations.'

'Which I imagine has been well taken care of,' one of the men commented.

'Naturally. Only a fool does anything that is not for personal profit. The weather machines will have to be located in various countries, countries that in themselves are quite satisfied with the weather they get, but must, nevertheless, have a machine so that it can contribute its own share to the whole quota of machines. To cut a long story short, gentlemen, I have made arrangements — have, in fact, got signed agreements — for machines to be erected in several countries. In all, there will be seven machines, with the master-machine situated in London here. The total cost of the machines alone will be in the neighborhood of tens of millions, without the labor involved in manufacturing, erecting and maintaining them.'

There was a silence. Rather gloomily the men around the table — those who represented finance at least — looked at each other. The scientists and engineers remained impersonal and obviously interested.

'The Denham Corp. will find the money,' Denham said. 'That is, with your approval.'

'I am not so sure that we can give that,' remarked Williams of 'Steel,' and one of the most influential men on the board of the Denham Corp. 'That is an enormous amount of money to fritter away on what may only be a dream.'

'Dream!' Denham echoed. 'Ridiculous! Richards and I have proven it to be an absolute fact, and I don't have to remind you, do I, that we are experienced scientists?'

'No, but . . . Why such expense? Why can't the countries involved pay for the machines that have to be in their countries? They'll derive benefit, won't they?'

'In most cases, yes. Here and there, as I have said, there are certain countries who don't want any change, but are, nevertheless, agreeable to a machine being erected to complete the chain . . . Getting back to the financial aspect, gentlemen. If we pay the whole price of the installation, we are not beholden to anybody. That's obvious. And how that works will become clear when I explain our tariff.'

'Tariff?' Williams of 'Steel' gave a start. 'What sort of tariff?'

'The scale of charges for any particular weather in any particular country at any particular time. According to what particular kind of weather is required, so will the charge be adjusted. It will, of course, demand greater resources on our part to produce, say, a cloudburst than it will to produce a prolonged spell of sunny weather. All corporations have their tariff, for electrical energy and so forth, and so, of course, shall we.'

Williams sat down and pondered, not quite sure of himself. But Denham was — completely.

'Suppose, for the moment, we leave the financial side out of the business,' he said. 'I'll explain it thoroughly later — why it is better that we finance everything and collect all the fees which will become due to us. I want to make clear the technical side. As I have said — seven machines. The subsidiary ones will be located in eastern Russia, in Kamchatka on the shores of the Sea of Okhotsk; in Australia in the region of New South Wales; in the Bouvet Islands, in the Southern Ocean — which was a matter for Norway to decide since they own them — on Easter island in the Pacific Ocean; in northern Canada near the Great Bear Lake; and in Spitzbergen in the Arctic Ocean, which again was the concern of Norway. Those six points represent a rough circle on a flat projection map of the globe, and they are so placed — taking the London machine as the governor-position — that they will influence the main atmospheric currents of the weather from and to every part of the world. When all the machines are in operation the weather will no longer be left to chance, to destroy, blister or flood the countryside. It will do as it is told, and wherever it is told, in any part of the Earth.'

'And the Governments of the various countries have signified their willingness for machines to be built on their territory?' another of the money men inquired.

'Definitely.' Denham indicated the desk with its letters and documents. 'There is the proof, gentlemen. Actually, since these other countries have agreed for us to build machines within their territories, they become part of the whole grand scheme, or corporation. For that reason I suggest our proposed company — which will be a branch of the Denham organization at root — should be called Climate Incorporated. At the head of this company will be myself, as the original inventor, and our chief scientist who will be responsible for the efficient working of the machines, will be Mr. Richards here.'

'That of course is a matter to be put to the vote,' commented Williams of 'Steel.' 'For my own part I am still more interested in the financial details than the scientific mumbo-jumbo. What assurance can you give us that the dues will be paid, or that some particular country will not wreck the machine within its borders if the weather required does not material-ize? Such a thing *could* happen.'

'It could,' Denham agreed, and then he

smiled grimly, 'but there's a particularly good reason why it wouldn't. What do power companies do if their bills are not paid?'

'Cut off the power, of course.'

'Exactly. We shan't do that, but we will prevent weather control from operating over that particular area. That will mean that the atmospheric pressures held back from that particular region by the influence of our machines will suddenly assert themselves over the region which has not paid. I don't quite know what the result would be, but according to my calculations, and Richards', devastation would be produced. The country concerned would lie in ruins! There can be no two ways about this business, gentlemen. Those involved must pay up, or be destroyed.'

'It won't work,' Williams said grimly. 'It's dictatorship, by way of weather! I never heard anything like it.'

'You mean you never heard anything so imaginative, so vast in its scope,' Denham retorted. 'Why, gentlemen, consider the business!' he went on, thumping the table. 'We're men of the world, not to be swayed by silly sentiments. The whole mass of civilization itself is built up on weather. Races have evolved as they have because of the weather. Then, turn the picture over and examine it. Everything, in some form or other, relies on the climate for its advancement — from the trifling flight of an airplane from one country to another, to the movement of global wars. Hold the weather, and we hold the whip hand.'

'Which means, in the end, that Climate Incorporated could dictate terms to anybody in the world,' Williams remarked bluntly.

'Such a possibility had occurred to me. The idea is only in its infancy as yet: the ramifications are endless.'

'And not very likeable either,' Williams snapped. 'I still say it is dictatorship, with flood and disaster if our terms are not accepted. You can't hold a gun at the head of the public like that — at least not with my connivance. I'm pulling out, before this thing gets out of hand!'

And Williams did just that. He picked

up his briefcase and left the boardroom without another word. For a moment the others looked uncertain; then Denham came back into the fray with his usual assurance.

'Evidently our good friend fails to appreciate the powerful position in which we intend to place ourselves,' he remarked. 'However, there may be others of like mind. If so, let's weed them out.'

Therein Denham started something that resulted after explosive argument in the retirement of two more board members. After that things settled down again, even if the conference did take nearly five grueling hours to complete itself. And in the end Denham won — got the required sanction to go ahead with his schemes. On balance it was quite obvious, from the way Denham put it anyhow, that the profits would be colossal, and anyhow the authority that Climate Incorporated could wield was definitely not to be ignored.

The meeting broke up in the early evening with Denham entirely content, but he did not rest there. He retreated from the scene of battle only to have a meal, then in the evening he was back again in his office, arranging engineering and labor details for the weather machines along with Richards. Though they had most of the facts and requirements to start with, it still took them until midnight to produce a working plan. With this in his charge Richards at last departed and Denham relaxed in his chair and lighted a cigar . . . The future, from where he sat, looked very rosy.

4

A dream realized

Through the months which followed, from early summer to winter and through to summer again — and a dull and dismal June — Richards, in charge of operations, acquitted himself magnificently. Always a good scientist and engineer, he rose to new heights with the entire onus of constructing the weather machines being placed upon him.

Labor forces were duly recruited in Russia, in Australia, in the Southern Ocean, on Easter Island, in Canada, and in Spitzbergen, and where recruitment was difficult, special forces were flown direct from London. Denham allowed nothing to stand in the way, and as far as London-control was concerned he supervised this task himself.

Naturally, the building of the machines was accompanied by the biggest publicity campaign ever. Denham got a good man to handle the job, and the result was that every stage of the building, from the Arctic to the Pacific, was covered by newspapers, television and radio commentaries. There was not a man or woman who did not know that weather control was definitely coming. By the time winter was again round the corner it would probably be an established fact.

Not far from the Denham Engineering organization in London there gradually grew an enormous ultramodern building of skyscraping proportions. In the early stages a gigantic hoarding named the edifice as the site of Climate Incorporated, a sign that in late June became transferred to a gigantic neon sign on top of the building itself. It gave Denham a warm glow of pleasure when he surveyed the edifice. In the ground floor and basements of the building were the controls, maps, and everything necessary to make contact with the subsidiary stations scattered about the world, while the upper regions contained all the offices and executive departments. The only people who looked on this masterpiece with some misgivings were the meteorologists themselves. What exactly was going to happen to them when weather forecasting was no longer necessary?

Denham considered it a special dispensation of Providence that, on the whole, the summer in England was a poor one. It lent added point, if any were needed, to the fact that weather control was a necessity. And when the miserable June gave way to the wettest July and August in living memory he was completely jubilant. If ever a man had reason for what he was doing, he had.

From June to September, although the machines were completed and ready for action, there was still a lot of detail to be worked out on the clerical side. Tariffs had to be fixed and agreed to, the particular type of weather wanted by any one country had to be booked and adhered to — for one year ahead — and in England an act of Parliament had to be passed legalizing weather control, after which various bodies put in their own claims for the type of weather required.

Those most representative were the Farmers' Union, and the Hotel and Boarding House associations, both of whom were the direct victims of any bad weather when, normally, it ought to be fine.

Out of all this mass of detail Denham and his board finally decided — for a year ahead — to produce a mild autumn, to be changed on December 1 to cold, dry weather with increasingly bitter winds, terminating on Christmas Day with a snowfall, just to be traditional. From Boxing Day to New Year a mild spell was agreed upon, and from Jan. 1 to March 21 cold, dry weather was to prevail . . . Wet conditions would exist until April 5, then would come a slow transition to correct summer. Any blizzards, cloudbursts, severe frosts, or other vagaries simply would not happen. Such was the program for the British Isles, only one unit in the worldwide pool of requirements, all of which were worked out in detail until at last the great plan was ready.

On Sept. 12, ready to launch the

scheme he had so ruthlessly stolen from Alvin Brook, Denham went to the microphones and television cameras to make his preliminary announcement — and most of the world listened to him, or the interpretation of his words into the appropriate language.

Nicholas Sutherland was one of the millions who watched Denham's complacent face on the television screen. He smoked his cigar and listened to what the tycoon had to say, while in the back of his mind many thoughts were crowding, thoughts that would one day find sudden and unexpected action.

'Today we are facing a new era in the history of civilization,' Denham said, somewhat grandiloquently. 'An era as important as radio, television, rocket flight, nuclear energy, and all the marvels that go to make up the background of our lives. We are about to end forever the perpetual menace of the weather, which — on balance — is far more our enemy than our friend. From the Arctic Circle to the Equator we have the weather on a leash, and in a moment or two that leash will tighten, and ever afterwards be held. Today marks the end of disaster by weather, the end of floods, hurricanes, and violent storms. Because this last physical enemy has been tamed, ships will no longer face the tempests, farming lands will no longer be unproductive, and the average man and woman will no longer find their summer holidays ruined by unexpected downfalls of moisture. Parliament is shortly to issue a calendar of weather, stating what type of weather will apply at particular times of the year, and in due course the calendar will probably be produced in every country in the world . . .

'We do not expect everybody will be happy about weather control,' Denham proceeded, with somewhat doubtful modesty. 'There will be one or two who will curse it. Certain bodies will arise and say we have no right to tamper — to which I can only say that man has tampered with everything else, so why not the weather? Certain bodies, even, will become extinct through Climate Incorporated, and will have to be absorbed into new fields. That is inevitable — as inevitable as the chaos that resulted among musicians when the talking picture first came out. Be that as it may, weather control is here, and will remain. My duty is to start the main London-control, and simultaneously every subsidiary station in the world will start action. For two days there may be disturbances, then the balance will settle and you will see for yourselves the benefit which can be derived.'

Denham turned from the cameras and the screens gave a long view of him stepping down from the specially constructed rostrum in the London-control powerhouse from which he had been speaking. He began moving towards a wilderness of apparatus, dominated by dials, switches and world-charts. Around him, white-coated technicians waited in respectful and somewhat self-conscious array.

'This,' Denham said, as the cameras tracked in to isolate him, 'is the switch which will bring weather control into being. I shall count six, and then plunge it into position.'

His massive paw clamped around a red-handled switch and he began to count steadily. The cameras moved in yet again to pick up the lever and hand.

' . . . three — four — five — six.'

Denham closed the switch. There was an outburst of sparks, and that was all — or nearly all. The microphones picked up a bass humming as the various machines in the great powerhouse started into action.

And to various parts of the world, moving with the speed of light, flashed invisible energy that started the subsidiary machines. Technicians watched their meters with unblinking eyes; muscular hands grasped vital switches.

Everywhere, from the freezing cold of the Arctic to the soft warmth of the Pacific ocean, the machines sprang into life. They gathered power, transmitting their invisible influence into the atmosphere, bringing about the dream which man has cherished for ages untold — control of the weather.

5

Hell let loose

Denham had said two days of disturbance, and he had not exaggerated. For two days the people of the world wondered what was happening. The darkness of midnight descended over the blazing regions of the Sahara Desert, suffocating warmth invaded the Arctic Circle, while deluging rain of a violence never before known descended on Italy. In the British Isles a gale arose and fast became a hurricane, leveling trees, tearing up buildings, even lifting traffic high in the screaming air and then smashing it down again. While in New Zealand there was an utter dead calm. In Australia there was a thunderstorm more violent than any volcanic eruption, and in the United States, San Francisco was literally buried under an avalanche of hailstones.

Then gradually the freak conditions

began to adjust themselves. Radio and telephone reported the weather back to London-control from all over the world — and as the man-made currents began to affect the atmospheric drifts the story was one of 'according to plan.' Each country was settling into the kind of weather for which it had asked. Over the British Isles, as the third day came, there spread a gentle mildness with a soft southerly wind. Overhead, an autumn sun gleamed pleasantly from a sky of cloudless blue. It was delightful, even if it was somehow phony. Long-suffering Britons just couldn't get the hang of Californian conditions in their normally haywire climate.

Be that as it may, the conditions remained. Day followed day, and every one was soft and warm and sunny, with the same gentle breeze blowing directly on the governed path from the distant shores of the Mediterranean. Those people who could take time off from work indulged again in a holiday, to make up for the disappointments they had received during the 'summer.' And, of course, this second vacation was a perfect success. One could not go wrong. No rain, no unpleasant chill, calm days and placid nights.

Everywhere it was the same. Every country was getting the weather it had ordered. Seven machines kept at bay the natural currents of the atmosphere, dissolving them or augmenting them according to the requirements of the country over which they would normally pass.

In Britain there were already signs of commercial upheaval, apparent by mid-October, with the weather conditions exactly the same as they had been in September. The first people to complain — even as Denham had foreseen — were the meteorologists. They were no longer needed. The radio and television stations, to say nothing of sea and air traffic, no longer needed their forecasts. The Met men were definitely forgotten men, with their maps unchanged week after week, the atmosphere entirely clear of all disturbances. Britain, and half Europe on one side and the Atlantic on the other, lay under the beneficent influence of a colossal and non-diminishing anticyclone.

The Met men made protests to Parliament and even organized marches complete with banners — not only in England, but in every country where weather forecasting had been a feature of daily life. They achieved a negative result. They had no protection in law, and they certainly had not got public sympathy. Too many people — wrongfully, be it said — remembered the time when incorrect forecasts had been given. The public laughed in the faces of the Met men, and this body of trained individuals was forced into other modes of livelihood. One by one the Met stations closed down.

Here, then, were the first casualties. Others followed in quick succession. Curiously enough, rainwear manufacturers went out of business in dozens. Rain would come, of course, when scheduled, but most of the manufacturers relied on it being an almost constant thing — in England, anyway — and the brief wet season shown on the parliamentary weather calendar did not at all justify the maintenance of big rainwear factories. So the casualty list increased, with only a few multiple firms remaining to supply the demand.

Among the farming communities there were endless debates on how to cash in on clockwork, infallible weather — and out of it there emerged new commercial enterprises for the growing of semi-tropical fruits as easily as tomatoes had formerly been grown.

From a general feeling of unreality and uncertainty a new spirit was born as November came in and the weather still remained unchanged. Calm, still, and sunny. The only difference lay in the rapidly shortening days, which, of course, had nothing to do with the weather anyhow.

Two who took advantage of the perfect conditions, along with millions of others, were young David Brook and his Aunt Dora. Now completely absorbed into Dora Lester's family, David nevertheless wondered, in his young mind, what had transpired to so completely remove his

with the matter-of-fact sagacity of youth he said:

'I think they're dead.'

'David! How can you say such a thing?'

'Because I believe it. I know they would never go away for so long and never send me a letter or something . . . ' David scrambled to his feet out of the grass and stood close to Dora, looking at her intently. 'What's happened to them, Aunty Dora? Why can't you tell me? I'm not a little boy any more, you know. On my next birthday I'll be fifteen.'

'Yes . . . you will at that.' It came as a surprise to Dora when she realized how the time had flown. 'I suppose you're old enough to know the facts — but even when I give them to you they don't mean much. I don't half understand it myself.'

'Let me hear them, anyway,' David suggested.

'All right. In June last year your father went to see a big engineering man in the city, and your mother followed him — on the same day. They were seen to go into this engineering man's office but nobody ever saw them come out. They've just disappeared, but that's no reason to suppose that they're dead.'

'If they're not dead, where are they? They'd have come home, wouldn't they?'

'I suppose so,' Dora agreed. 'David, I just don't understand it. When your mother left you with me, after telling me where she was going, she said she'd only be an hour or two — and I've never seen her since. Or your father either.'

David said slowly: 'Dad showed me a box thing be had with a sort of lens on the top. I remember how, one evening, he stopped a rainstorm with it. Come to think of it, on a big scale, the sort of weather we've got now could be made by the box thing on a big scale. Has this new firm of Climate In-something-or-other got anything to do with the weather?'

'It has everything to do with it. They make the weather so that it is perfect all the time. Haven't you seen that in the newspapers?'

'Sort of,' David admitted. 'But the papers are too dry to read. Look, aunty, this engineering man dad went to see. Who was it? What was his name?'

'Marcus Denham.'

David started. 'But that's the same name as the man who's head of Climate Thingummy.'

'Yes, same man,' Dora assented, wondering where the boy's imagination was going to carry him.

'Then there's something funny,' David decided, his young face peculiarly grim. 'Dad takes him a weather box on a small scale, mother follows after him, and nobody hears about them any more . . . After that weather control on a big scale turns up. All this is *dad's* idea. It has nothing to do with Marcus Denham.'

'No doubt everything was legally arranged,' Dora said rather fearfully. She was remembering the plans and drawings of Alvin Brook that she had cleared from his house before letting it out to rent, the income from which was helping with David's education and upbringing. At the present time they were stored in a trunk with other possessions. She was intending to pass them to David when he was older. 'I agree that weather control is very like your dad's idea, but — '

'There just aren't any buts,' David said simply. 'It's the same thing, on a big scale, and I shan't rest until I know where dad and mum are.'

'But, dear, there's nothing you can do. The police are doing all they can, and we mustn't interfere.'

'No, I suppose not,' David agreed, but to Dora it was plain he was only speaking words. At the back of his mind he meant to do a good deal . . . but not just yet. He was too young for that.

And, about this time, Marcus Denham himself was in the midst of a meeting with Nicholas Sutherland. He had not asked for it: Sutherland had simply presented himself, and for once his child-like geniality was absent. He looked — and was — decidedly grim.

'What's the idea, Denham?' he asked bluntly, tossing an immaculate hat on Denham's big desk.

'Idea?' Denham raised his eyebrows, his florid face somewhat hostile. 'For that matter, I might ask you the same question. You come in here without being asked and — '

'I don't need to ask. We're old enemies, aren't we, and drop in on one another when we feel like it?' Sutherland sat at the opposite side of the desk. 'I want to know what's behind this weather-control business.'

'Money,' Denham replied laconically. 'Or maybe you can think of a better reason?'

'How much does Alvin Brook get out of it?'

'What?' Instantly Denham was on his guard.

'Alvin Brook, the man who invented weather control. He seems to have become pretty quiet since his invention became a worldwide fact. I'd rather like to contact him.'

Denham said nothing. His mind was working fast, trying to find a clear path out of this unexpected difficulty.

'Why not put your cards on the table?' Sutherland suggested, relaxing a little. 'You may fool everybody else, Denham, including the police, but you're not fooling me. Alvin Brook has vanished, and so has his wife, and I'm pretty sure you know where they've gone . . . Or shall I put it more bluntly and say that you know where the bodies are?'

'What the hell!' Denham exploded, his face purpling. 'Do you dare to sit there and call me a murderer?'

'Yes — because I know exactly what kind of a man you are. You know a lot of things about which you haven't spoken, Denham. I'll let you remain tight-lipped on one condition — that you call off this weather-control dictatorship and let a group of men and women from varying countries handle it. That way it will no longer be the responsibility of one man.'

'I thrive on responsibility,' Denham said sourly.

'Maybe — but your exclusive control of things doesn't bode well for the rest of us. You've got too much power, and though you haven't used it to the full as yet, I've not the least doubt that you will do, when it suits you. It's got to stop.'

'Just because you say so? Do you think I'm an idiot?'

'No. I think you're clever — clever as a fox and as brutal as the devil . . . '

Sutherland grinned mirthlessly. 'You didn't know that Alvin Brook came to me with his invention before, presumably, coming to you, did you? I turned it down — but evidently you had greater vision.'

Denham did not say anything: he was too busy looking at danger lights. He had thought that only Nancy Brook knew of the invention, outside of the boy David, of course. And now it seemed that his worst enemy knew plenty, too.

'I'll tell you what I'm going to do,' Sutherland said. 'Either you have sense and make this weather-control business the affair of a select body of people, from whom we can rightfully expect impartial decisions — or else I'll tear up everything by the roots to prove you murdered Alvin Brook — or otherwise got him out of the way — and stole his idea. You can please yourself.'

Still Denham was silent, his small blue eyes fixed on Sutherland's grim face.

'Don't think I couldn't do it,' Sutherland added. 'It's a debatable point which of us has the most money and influence — you or me. Where you can sidetrack the public, and the police because they can only move within the limits prescribed by law, you just can't sidetrack me. I've wanted to have a go at you for a long time, Denham, and at last you've given me the opportunity.'

'If you think you're smart enough to whip me, you've got another think coming,' Denham snapped. 'I'll lick you, whatever you get up to.'

'We'll see.' Sutherland rose purposefully and took his hat from the desk. 'I'll give you a week to do as I suggest. If you haven't done anything by then you can look out for trouble.'

He turned toward the door as Denham sat glaring after him; then at the door he turned.

'And, Denham — Don't waste your time having your hired thugs watch my movements. I'm wise to them, and if they try anything like that they might end up in the same queer way as Alvin Brook and his wife.'

The door closed decisively, and Denham sat scowling in front of him, only just appreciating the tightness of the spot he was in. Even if he would not admit to himself he knew in his inmost heart that Sutherland was on: there were definitely no flies on that gentleman.

'This is Brook's fault,' Denham muttered. 'He distinctly said nobody else knew of his idea . . . Damn! There's got to be some way, and Sutherland's too fly to fall for any of the usual traps — and he's too influential a man to be eliminated in the ordinary way.'

Calming somewhat, he took a cigar out of the box and lit it. He pondered through a long interval then his eyes lighted somewhat as the germ of an idea struck him. He pressed a button on the intercom.

'Have Mr. Richards come in here a moment.'

'Yes, Mr. Denham.'

There was an interval of a few minutes, then the tall figure of the scientist entered. He glanced inquiringly as he came across to the desk.

'Something's come up,' Denham said briefly. 'You know as well as I do by this time that weather control isn't my own exclusive idea — '

'I've gathered that a lot of it was conceived by Alvin Brook,' Richards admitted, sitting down. 'After which Brook conveniently disappeared along with his wife.'

'Exactly. That's all anybody knows. Except one person, who also knows that the invention was really Alvin Brook's. He's turned awkward. He's going to turn everything inside out to prove the facts unless I agree to certain demands.'

'And what are the demands?' Richards asked calmly, entirely sure of his position as chief scientist of Climate Incorporated.

'That I relinquish absolute control of Climate Incorporated and turn it over to a body of various men and women, thereby making all decisions impartial. In a word, I am a dictator — according to Nicholas Sutherland, the one man who knows too much.'

'Nicholas Sutherland, eh? The oil tycoon?'

'The same — from which you'll see the extent of the danger. I refuse to give in to his demands, but I've also got to stop him investigating anything. The only way to do that is to — eliminate him.'

'That won't be easy, Mr. Denham. He's a big man.'

'There is a way, and it can never be classed as murder. If it's classed as anything at all, it will be 'misadventure.' It necessitates using weather control as an offensive weapon for the first time.'

'Oh?' Richards waited in puzzled interest.

'It is possible, as you know yourself, to produce localized weather conditions over any given spot. At will, heavy rain, frost, or a thunder or hailstorm can be created.'

'True,' the scientist admitted.

'Sutherland's home is in Essex — out in the country, a big rambling Georgian mansion. I've been to it once. It's quite isolated, with the nearest village about five miles away ... Now, suppose a terrific localized thunderstorm were to break over that spot? Suppose the mansion were destroyed, and Sutherland with it, by a bolt of lightning? Nobody could call that murder, could they?'

Richards was silent, thinking it out.

'It would happen at night,' Denham resumed. 'I'd have men make certain that Sutherland was home at the time.'

'What about his family? They'll be with him.'

'Unfortunately for them, yes. One can't discriminate.'

'There'll be snags,' Richards mused. 'To produce a storm violent enough to create the lightning effect you suggest a strong atmospheric cold front will have to be launched, and that will have to move across a warm area, specially created in that spot. The most violent storms are created on a cold front — or used to be before weather control. And the warm area will have to be created in the daytime.'

'All right — create one.' Denham shrugged. 'Then bring in the cold front at night. Since that will mean heavy cloud as the cold front progresses, it's better to do it at night so Sutherland will not have any indication of what's happening. He'll probably be asleep. Also, the storm won't hit anywhere else because it can't build up until it strikes the specially warm area around Sutherland's home.'

'Fantastic,' Richards muttered. 'To create a storm to kill a man. I don't think I ever realized before how deadly this control of the weather can be. And if it comes to that I'm not sure I want any part of it.'

Denham started. 'What did you say?'

'I don't like the idea of killing a man — and probably his family too — by means of remote controlled murder. That's what it is when you get down to the solid truth.'

Denham said: 'If you don't do this job, Sutherland will dig up everything he can and in the end Climate Incorporated will cease to exist, as far as I'm concerned anyhow. If I go you will too. We're facing a crisis, and we've got to act ruthlessly.'

'Supposing we follow out this idea of yours. Where's the guarantee that he won't escape?'

'There's no guarantee, but the chances are that we'll succeed. Obviously he will stop inside when there's a storm brewing, and it is almost a certainty that he'll be inside when the peak flash is reached which ought to destroy his home. I don't claim the idea's watertight, but it's as near as dammit.'

Richards thought for a moment, then he sighed a little and got to his feet.

'All right, Mr. Denham, I'll do as you ask. I'll chart the path of this localized storm, and then I'll release it when you give the word. All I have to be sure of is that he'll be at home when the blow falls.'

'I'll make sure of that,' Denham promised. 'I'll start right away and have Sutherland's movements watched. Even if he becomes aware of the surveillance, he won't be able to do anything about it. How long will it take you to chart the storm track?'

'Oh, about six hours. Let me know when to release it.'

On that the scientist left, still not at all sure that he ought to have anything to do with murder — but against that there was the unpleasant fact that Sutherland would use all his influence and money to break the hold Climate Incorporated was rapidly gaining. And that, even as Denham had pointed out, would probably mean one chief scientist looking for another job. Yes, it was probably best to destroy that possibility at the start.

So Denham and Richards both went to work, and naturally Nicholas Sutherland had no idea what was intended. He was certainly alert for any dirty business on the part of Denham's many strong-arm men — but the thought of a storm, specially created and driven in his direction, never remotely occurred to him . . . Which was the main reason why it succeeded.

A week later, following a cloudless day with heat abnormally oppressive in the Essex area, a storm broke over the county about 3 o'clock in the morning. It only lasted 30 minutes, but in that 30 minutes hell was let loose. Not a cottage, barn or house was left standing. Trees were felled by the hundreds and nearly dry brooks rose to over-flowing. At the close of the storm a cyclonic wind lifted the debris of buildings to the skies, and the first red light of dawn revealed a blackened and lightning-riven waste.

Dawn pilots, specially assigned by

Denham, explored the area and then came back to report. The mansion of Nicholas Sutherland had disappeared as though hit by a bomb. All that remained were a few blackened stones sunk deep in oozing mud.

* * *

The 'freak' storm over Essex disturbed public confidence quite a lot and, as he had expected, Denham had his hands full explaining away the disaster. His main line was that one of the machines had developed a fault, and before its rectification had been possible the storm had broken out. It was regrettable, of course, but just one of those things. Richards verified this theory and, in the end, the public accepted it because there was no other course.

So calmness returned, and the weather calendar was adhered to. From December 1 to Boxing Day biting winds and snowfalls were present, and from Boxing Day to New Year it was mild again. So on up the calendar scale to April 5, when the slow transition to ordered, perfect summer weather commenced. Apparently everything in the garden was lovely. There was no doubt now, after intensive inquiry, that Nicholas Sutherland had died in the Essex storm, so Denham was well satisfied that he had not a single dangerous enemy. Which in a sense was true — but other things were boiling up under the surface.

The ordered weather was both a benefit and a menace. That could be seen clearly now. The changed economic and social conditions that had existed at the outset of climatic control were now more pronounced than ever, and particularly in England, where a reliable climate had formerly been unknown.

On the one hand there were vast industrial changes: on the other the curious growing mental apathy of the British people. Normally geared to an eternal struggle with disturbed weather, temperament was undergoing a change to the more leisurely, drowsy attitude typical of the people of the Italian, Spanish, and Mediterranean countries. Keen business sense was lacking, and although it was a comparatively new innovation, weather control was commencing to present itself as a menace. This much the far-seeing ones already knew . . . but not Denham. He was quite satisfied, as well he might be, seeing the dues he was collecting and adding to his already colossal financial pile.

It was Spain who raised the first protest over weather control. Senor Vandarez, head of the Spanish equivalent of the trade unions, made a special visit to Britain in sun-soaked early May, and went direct to Denham's headquarters. Denham greeted him cordially, but his pleasantry soon vanished when he heard what the Spaniard had to say.

'Mr. Denham, my country requires a release from weather control.' Vandarez's English was nearly perfect, and his enthusiasm tremendous. 'Our climate has gone completely wrong since weather control came in, and we are not getting the kind of weather we asked for. We were better off before control of the climate was attempted. It would seem that your foul English weather has descended on us, and it is rapidly ruining our industries — which your country has assumed in competition with us.'

Denham frowned a little. 'I don't quite understand.'

'No? Surely it is simple? Our main industry was formerly the export of dates, oranges, pomegranates, rice, maize, ground-nuts, cotton, and so forth. Now that industry is fast vanishing due to the change in climate. Your country, on the other hand, is developing — during the summer months — the trade which belonged to us.' Vandarez stared at Denham anxiously. 'It cannot go on, Mr. Denham. As a country we shall become useless. Rain falls constantly on lands that have been always dry at this season. Once even we had snow. An unheard of thing!'

Denham shrugged. 'So you object, senor, because Britain has assumed industries usually assigned to sub-tropical climates? You object to our growing oranges and the rest of it? You imagine you have an exclusive right to a fair climate and constant sun?'

'No, Mr. Denham. We have no exclusive right, but we object to the conditions that now beset us. Rain, wind, even snow — at this most beautiful time of the year.'

Denham did not answer. Getting to his feet he went across to the enormous world-projection map on the far wall and studied it, then he turned and looked at the Spaniard.

'For your information, senor, you are getting a lot of the residue of atmospheric currents which normally would pass over England. You must realize that the countries most favored by Climate Incorporated are those in whose boundaries one of our climatic machines stand. It is not possible to please everybody, and you must realize that the unpleasant conditions have to go *somewhere*. Your country, and one or two others in Europe, are the unfortunate recipients of the depressions and troughs usually associated with British and west European countries.'

'We pay our dues to you for certain weather to be present,' Vanderez snapped.

'So far there has been no attempt to stick to your side of the bargain. That being so, no more dues will be paid, and I will take the matter of our ruined trade before the World Council of Trade for consideration. To you, Spain is just a name on a world map: to us it is everything. Our very lives . . . '

'We will do what we can to straighten things out,' Denham promised, at which Vandarez rose to his feet with a look of obvious contempt.

'I think you can save yourself the trouble, Mr. Denham. We of Spain intend to dissociate ourselves entirely from weather control, and all the evils that go with it.'

Vandarez departed, an extremely angry man. Denham stood for a while, looking down on London in the midst of its drowsy heat. His eyes traveled to the park-like space nearby where palm trees had recently been planted, and were flourishing. Even he was struck for a moment by the fantasy of it all. Sub-tropical England and inclement Spain. The old order had completely changed . . . Then he went over to the intercom and summoned Richards.

The scientist arrived in a few moments, his expression inquiring. He listened as Denham told him of Vandarez's complaint.

'What can you do about it?' Denham demanded. 'Spain itself is not so important in the scheme of things, but if other countries start complaining as well, we may soon find Climate Incorporated hasn't very strong foundations.'

Richards shrugged. 'Not much I can do, Mr. Denham, and you know that yourself. Spain, most of Northern Africa, and Libya, have become what we call tempest-spots. They receive the atmospheric currents, which our climate machines hold at bay. They are, so to speak, in the safety-valve region. You know as well as I do that we cannot completely block the natural winds and drifts without causing trouble, so certain regions — unimportant ones — have been assigned as tempest spots. Into these tempest spots pass the unwanted air currents and rain areas. Spain, North

Africa and Libya don't produce anything particularly useful to the world economy, nothing that we can't now produce ourselves, anyhow. So, they're redundant.'

'Why didn't you consult me before settling on these tempest spots?' Denham snapped.

'I hardly thought it necessary. There have to be a number of 'safety-valve' areas, otherwise control of the climate will be like corking up steam in a bottle. There are four other areas.'

'Four other areas, did you say? Four? Where are they?'

'The West Indies, Iceland, Northern Finland, and Northern Ireland. None of them produce anything worthwhile, or have any climatic machines on their territory, so it doesn't matter much if they become tempest spots.'

'That's only your own opinion, Richards! When all of them start complaining to the World Trade Council, I'll have to do some fast talking. We're supposed to be providing whatever climate is wanted, by whatever country. In the case of the West Indies, Iceland, Northern Ireland

and Spain — to say nothing of North Africa and Libya — that hasn't been done.'

'Then they must stop paying their dues,' Richards shrugged. 'We have got to have safety zones, and I chose those countries as the least likely to affect us in the general scheme of things . . . If climatic control were a complete thing it would be different — but it isn't. Absolute mastery of every zone on Earth is an impossibility, at present anyhow. We can only take those which are the most important.'

'All right, Richards, let it go . . . We'll see what happens.'

'Very well, sir.'

Richards went and Denham returned to his work with a distinctly uneasy feeling. The thought that climatic control was not one hundred per cent efficient in every part of the world was something of a shock. He wondered what the World Trade Council would have to say when Senor Vanderez laid his complaint before them.

In a little under a month Denham found out what the Council thought — in no uncertain terms. Climate Incorporated was, in fact, deemed to be an illegal organization, in that it operated in parts to the detriment of countries and their livelihood. Denham was ordered to present himself before the Council and explain his plans for the future — particularly his plans for the countries that were suffering as Spain was.

He protested violently, he had lawyer Carlow try — vainly — to sweep aside the Council's orders. He tried everything he could think of — but to no avail. To the Council he had to go, a great building of white stone in Rio de Janeiro, within which all the trade difficulties and arbitrations of every country were decided.

Here — treated with every courtesy but feeling very much like a prisoner — Denham was taken to task. He was not exactly on trial, but he certainly had to explain everything to grave-faced judges whose job it was to interpret everything from the angle of international law.

The back-and-forth wrangling between international lawyers and something that

Denham could not properly understand. Things only made sense when the supreme judge of the World Trade Council summed everything up.

'Mr. Denham, the issue is plain. Through climatic control, of which you are the head and responsible authority, the countries of Spain and Libya, and half of Northern Africa, have lost their normal climate and become rain-sodden wildernesses. Because of that, trade and livelihood have gone too . . . It is up to you to recompense those countries to the full. You will also restore their normal climate to them. And keep it maintained. If you do not, this Council will request the various Governments of the world to act in concert against you and secure the closing down of Climate Incorporated. Have you, at this stage, anything you wish to say?'

'Only one thing,' Denham retorted arrogantly. 'I do not intend to allow countries like Spain, Libya and Africa to upset plans which are intended for the benefit of the world at large. That the majority should be jeopardized by the grumbling of the minority is unthinkable, and I won't tolerate it!'

'As you wish. Mr. Denham. You have our edict, and our warning, and you know enough of the strength of the World Trade Council to appreciate that we can put our warnings into action. There is nothing more to be said and, for the moment, the matter is closed.'

Upon which Denham returned to London — a hot, dusty London. He was in a foul temper, particularly furious that any tinpot Council should dare to dictate to him . . . Only it was *not* tinpot: it was immensely powerful. And that was the point that bothered him.

For a long time after his return he weighed up the chances against him, and arrived at the unpleasant conclusion that they were extremely heavy. He surveyed the climatic map, the position of the tempest zones, and finally he rang for Richards.

Richards came in a few moments, as unruffled as ever. He took a seat at the desk as Denham motioned.

'Trouble, sir?' Richards inquired.

'Definitely. And big trouble ... ' Denham related what had happened at the Council meeting. The scientist listened and then shrugged.

'I don't see what you can do, Mr. Denham.'

'I've got to do something. I've got to restore normal conditions to Spain, Libya and North Africa. If I don't the consequences will be disastrous. The Council has enough power to turn Governments against me, and once that happens Climate Incorporated is as good as done for ... I've been studying the map,' Denham went on, nodding to it. We've got to shift the 'safety zone' areas from their present position and locate them somewhere else.'

'That won't be easy,' Richards replied. 'Everything is just in balance at the moment.'

'That I know — but a change has got to be made. For instance — what about the Arctic and Antarctic regions? Why can't there be 'safety zones' there? Those areas are just wilderness.'

Richards got up and studied the map

from a distance; then he nodded slowly.

'Yes, I suppose it could be done, but it will mean a good deal of diversion for the established drifts. I chose the West Indies, Iceland, Spain, and so forth because they were the most convenient locations for the general setup.'

'Then change it,' Denham ordered. 'And quickly. The annoying part, to my mind, is that there should have to be 'safety valves' at all. We'll have to see if we can't work something out to make the atmospheric circuit complete.'

Richards shook his head slowly. 'I'm afraid we'll not manage that, Mr. Denham. The Earth and its normal atmosphere and wind drift will always remain, no matter how we try to mould the conditions to our own uses. We must allow an outlet, or there'll be a disaster.'

'Yes, you're probably right, Richards.' Denham gave a gloomy nod. 'All right, we'll have to take things as we find them. Get busy on these new safety areas right away.'

'O.K.'

Richards departed to carry out orders,

and they necessitated he personally visit all the countries where subsidiary machines were located. It was a long job switching everything around, and for a while at least it altered the balance of weather the world over. Unexpected storms broke out, deluges swamped sun-soaked Britain: Canada became the recipient of the most amazing fog in its history. From one end of the country to the other a dense, humid blanket descended and remained for three days, in which time almost total paralysis of traffic occurred.

Then, slowly, as the machines began to force new atmospheric patterns, the pleasant conditions of yore were gradually established. England returned to its semi-tropical status; Canada basked in a not-too-hot summer. America smiled under perfect weather — and to Spain there came the burning sun and cloudless sky to which it was accustomed. The rains and gales departed from North Africa and Libya, and the West Indies, Iceland and Northern Ireland emerged from the climatic chaos that had temporarily been their lot as the 'safety valve' countries.

In a word, everybody was satisfied once more. Radio, television and newspapers proclaimed the fact; and with the realization of it Denham began to relax again, aware how closely he had come to a major disaster . . .

Even so, things were not perfect — not by any means. But the troubles now were small enough for Denham to deal with them in his own way — and they were mostly located in Britain. For instance, as June blazed into July, and July gave way to an insufferably hot August under cloudless skies there arose a deputation of medical men who took their complaints direct to Denham himself. He listened to them politely, vaguely astonished at the nature of their harassment.

'You may not realize it, Mr. Denham,' the spokesman said, 'but there are sides to this climatic control which you may never have thought of. Something's got to be done, even if Parliament have to enforce it. Do you know that doctors are having to work overtime, with hardly a break, dealing with cases of severe sunburn and heat prostration?'

'I am sure the medical fraternity is dealing with it most efficiently,' Denham commented, smiling complacently.

'True enough, but the British people are not made by Nature to stand up to constant tropical heat! They behave just as they did when the climate was variable. They wander and lie around in the blazing sun without hats and suffer disastrously in consequence. For three months now, without a break, the mean temperature has been around ninety degrees Fahrenheit.'

'True — and it will remain like that, unbroken, until the end of November. Parliament has decreed it. It's not a bit of use complaining, gentlemen. The only thing to do is for one of you prominent medical men to make a speech on television, telling the masses how to behave in a tropical climate. I will willingly grant you free time on my network to do it. Otherwise, if the masses are such fools as to expose themselves to danger, I'm afraid they must take the consequences.'

'That's not a very charitable outlook,'

the medical man snapped, mopping his brow.

'I agree — but then I don't pretend that I am a charitable man. I'm controlling a worldwide climatic organization, and it is impossible to alter things for the misfit minority. Everything, from commerce to people, has changed since weather control came in. I'm afraid there's nothing I can do, gentlemen.'

And as far as Denham was concerned, that ended it. A few days later, on the Denham television network, one of the doctors did give a speech on preventative measures, but how much effect it had was doubtful . . . Perhaps the smartest doctor of the lot was the one who resigned his profession and instead started a small factory for the manufacture of tropical clothing. He set himself dead in line for making a fortune.

These internal changes in the country were of course inevitable. In twelve months Britain's exports had completely changed — or rather been added to, by the inclusion of tropical and semi-tropical fruits. Fortunes were being made in this direction, just as other fortunes were tottering.

Curiously enough, the book trade had a tremendous fillip. Where people had formerly remained indoors to watch television, the furious heat now drove them outside and this demanded some relaxation with no effort attached. Book publishers, saved from the doldrums, started to reap fortunes.

From other countries too there were reports of general changes, and on the whole climatic control seemed to be more liked than disliked. At least one could rely on what was going to happen, and the threat of sudden storms, hurricanes, and floods had gone forever . . .

Yet perfection had not been achieved. There was always something in the background, liable to cause trouble — and because he was at the center of this spider's web of climatic control, Marcus Denham was the first to hear about it . . . It was nearing the end of the bleaching summer — late August to be exact — when he received a shock.

Richards came into the office one

morning, his habitual calm ruffled.

'Are you at liberty for a moment, Mr. Denham?'

'Surely.' Denham looked up from his desk. He was working in air-conditioned coolness, the shades down across the sunlit windows. 'Anything wrong?'

'I'm afraid so. There may be plenty of trouble blowing up.'

'What! Again?' Denham gave a groan. 'I thought we'd got everything ironed out.'

Richards hurried over to the projection map, talking as he went.

'It's about the 'safety-valve' areas. Things aren't working out at all well. I've just been looking through the reports of the pilots who maintain a constant run over the climatic courses. It seems that the Arctic and Antarctic regions have ceased to exist as such, and there's an enormous evacuation south and north of peoples living on the fringe of the Arctic and Antarctic Circles.'

Richards picked up the pointer and traced it along the northernmost edges of Asia, Alaska, Canada, Greenland, Sweden and Russia in the northern half of the globe; and along the small islands fringing — and in — the Antarctic Circle in the south.

'The evacuation in the south is negligible owing to the small population,' Richards resumed. 'But in the north it's serious. Whole masses of people, with their belongings are driving into the more settled regions of Canada and America on the one hand, and Central Europe and Asia on the other.'

'But what for?' Denham demanded. 'What are they running away from?'

'Tidal waves, floods, and tempest. The oceans that formerly were ice have melted and the water has spilled over on to the land. The 'safety-valve' areas have become a wilderness of churning sea, mild air, and terrific tempests in which nothing can live — not under the former frozen conditions, anyhow. There isn't a cold spot anywhere on the Earth, and we can't divert air currents again to produce freezing conditions in north and south, because that would again demand new 'safety-valve' spots. It's going to be hard to cope with this mass evacuation from the 'safety-valve' centers.'

'We'll manage it somehow,' Denham decided. 'It's all included in the general pattern change which climatic control brings about. We just can't help it. The evacuees will have to be absorbed into the communities of the countries into which they've traveled.'

'All right,' Richards said worriedly. 'Let's hope it works out that way.'

As it happened, it did, and Denham breathed a sigh of relief. Somehow, the various governments of Canada, America, Europe and Asia managed to find room for the flood of evacuees, even if they did so under protest. There was talk for a time of doing away with climatic control, until it was found that too many big businesses relied on its continuance — after which nothing more was heard about the matter. Once again Denham had weathered a crisis, but there was deepened within him the uneasy feeling that one day something of really lethal proportions would arise which would snatch climatic control out of his hands.

He got through the perfect autumn without trouble, but with the coming of winter and its icy, governed calmness, there came evidence of fresh trouble — this time from air and shipping companies. And, actually, there was warning of trouble some time before the air and shipping authorities took notice of it. The warning lay in the amazing displays, on the winter side of earth, of the Aurora Borealis and Australis. The Borealis, for example, was visible each night as far south as Sierra Leone, on the west coast of Africa, beating even the record visibility of January, 1938, when the Borealis had been seen clearly as far south as Madeira.

There had to be a reason for it, even more so as it was repeated night after night, and in the southern regions the displays from the Australis were just as phenomenal. Ships at sea, and aircraft, reported that both disturbances were visible as mighty draperies of varicolored fire blotting out the heavens.

Puzzled by the reports, Denham and Richards surveyed the spectacle from a private plane, and then returned to discuss the matter and reduce it to its scientific implication.

'I don't somehow get the impression it's dangerous,' Denham said, debating the view of the auroral lights, visible even now through the lofty office window.

'No, they're not dangerous,' Richards admitted. 'And the cause of them isn't far to seek. They'll be with us as long as climatic control operates.'

'Why will they?' Denham turned from the window.

'Because they're created — or rather augmented — by the magnetic-electrical currents which we are sending into the atmosphere to control the climate. Normally the auroras appear after magnetic storms or sunspot activity, but in these days we're producing a constant flow of vibration and electrical radiation into the atmosphere . . . so they're just another concomitant of climatic control.'

'And a very beautiful one,' Denham reflected. 'The tourist agencies might make something out of this. We've already got a magnificent tourist traffic to our 'tropical England,' but we have the added attraction of the auroral lights during the winter months, thanks to our northerly latitude. Mmm, I must see if something can't be done about it.'

His business sense was definitely aroused, particularly so as he had a personal stake in most of the tourist agencies in the country — but his idea never came to fruition because the display of auroral draperies also had another meaning — and not a beautiful one either . . . It was next day that the air and shipping lines had something to say.

Compasses were useless in practically all oceans. At first the variation had been slight and not enough to cause trouble, but now the electrical disturbances in the atmosphere were obviously building up into something sinister. Radio, too, was nearly impossible to hear. Pilots of airplanes and commanders of ships were groping — groping — groping, under skies that blazed with a million colors. The ships sailed oceans that were always calm, where gales were unknown, where overhead amidst the stars there blazed these softly shifting curtains of multi-colored light.

To what avail, when compasses were haywire and radio could hardly be received or transmitted? Planes, too, flying through the calmness of night and day, freed forever from the perils of icing or thunderstorms, never touched by a cloud, were nonetheless in danger because radio signals would not come properly through the electricity-sodden atmosphere, and compasses were likewise off balance.

Governments held conferences. Denham waited for the outcome, knowing from press and television that a good deal of trouble was threatening. What decision the governments would have reached he did not know, for before they could make up their minds something happened to settle the issue.

A storm broke unexpectedly over the placid west coast of America and pro-ceeded thereafter to tear its way on a 50-mile track right across the United States, traveling thence into the broad, becalmed Atlantic. The moment he heard news of the storm's outbreak in the Pacific ocean, a few miles west of San Francisco, Denham got in touch with Richards — and remained in touch while radio announced the storm's progress at tremendous speed to the eastern side of America.

'But what's gone wrong?' Denham demanded of Richards, once he had him on the phone. 'Where did the storm come from? From the latest report there's a 90-mile-an-hour wind, accompanied by torrential rain, lightning and thunder. It just couldn't happen if you're doing your job properly.'

'I'm doing my job to the best of my ability, Mr. Denham,' Richards retorted. 'Right now I'm at London Control headquarters, trying to find out what's happened. The only information I can gather is that the sub-station on Easter Island has reported a fault in their northerly drift control. That could mean that the general pressure has dropped all along the western side of the Americas and Canada, resulting in the formation of a depression — which, in the manner of currents before climatic control — is now travelling eastwards and wreaking hurricane havoc as it goes.'

'It's disastrous!' Denham snapped. 'Do something quick!'

'I'll do what I can, but I'm not a magician.'

'Which way is the thing headed, anyhow? If it's moving east toward the Atlantic, what's to stop it striking us?'

'Nothing. We'll have to be prepared. I don't know which way it's going because there are no Met men in existence any more. I'll see if the stations in Spitzbergen and the Bouvet Islands can do anything. Perhaps a deflecting current can be swung toward the disturbance.'

Richards switched off and went to work. Denham switched off, too, and compressed his lips. He looked out of the window on to the brittle brightness of the winter day; then he turned again to the radio. It was still chattering the news of the great storm sweeping across the American states and leaving a trail of utter destruction in its wake.

Only afterwards was the full extent of the damage known, the cost soaring into billions of dollars. Trees and buildings were uprooted wholesale, entire cities were damaged by wind and lightning, great areas of agricultural land were several feet under water, and the cost in human life was staggering. A giant's knife had split America from San Francisco to New York. No storm that had ever been experienced had been a tenth of the fury of this one.

And only just in time was the havoc stopped before it reached England. In mid-Atlantic the resources of the Spitzbergen and Bouvet Islands stations came into action to project a v-shaped counter-current, which filled in the atmospheric depression. As a result, calm spread its beneficent mantle. But the memory remained and Climate Incorporated was the scapegoat.

American confidence was shaken to its depths, and the American people did not take long to convey their impressions to other countries. Climatic control was an idiot's dream: it had cost the American people untold dollars and thousands of lives, and it would take years to make good the damage of a few hours. Better to take the normal risks of inclemency than this.

Climate Incorporated must make reparation. The organization couldn't escape under the clause 'Act of God'. The whole thing had happened through a machine breakdown, which in fact scientist Richards had to admit when the inquiry was complete.

6

Dictatorship

The invective poured on Denham nearly broke him in the days around Christmas and New Year — and to it was added the air and shipping complaints concerning incorrect compasses and faulty radio. Finally, as the governing director of Climate Incorporated, Denham was compelled to appear before the international court — at which each nation was represented — and stand trial. The defending counsel was Carlow, and he only did it for the money he could get out of it. Even so, Denham looked calm enough as he faced his accusers. His bulldog courage would not let him look defeated, even if he was.

'Marcus Denham,' the International Prosecutor said, 'you are indicted here on a charge of willful misrepresentation. You have led the governments of the world to believe that you have a system of climatic control that could bring nothing but benefit. That hardly fits in with the disaster that has recently befallen the United States, nor with the delays and losses incurred by sea and shipping lines through useless compasses . . . We do not blame you for the magnetic influences apparent at both poles of the Earth, but we *do* blame you for not having foreseen the snags in your so-called perfect climatic system.'

Denham did not say a word. He left it to Carlow to do all the talking — but, brilliantly though Carlow spoke, it was plain that judge and jury were not impressed . . . Through many days the trial of Marcus Denham dragged on, until at last the jury found him guilty. Thereupon the judge made his pronouncement.

'Marcus Denham, you have been tried and found guilty of acting in a manner unfavorable to the various countries of the world. Naturally, since this is not a normal case, nor an ordinary law court, there can be no question of you being sentenced to a term of imprisonment. That is not within my jurisdiction. But what I can — and shall — do is inflict the maximum penalty within my power. Take notice, therefore, Marcus Denham, that all climatic machines, in all countries, will be immediately dismantled, and a special detachment of scientists under London authority will take charge of, and dismantle, the London-control headquarters. You, on the other hand, as governing director of Climate Incorporated, will make reparations to the United States government in the sum of twenty billion dollars, the calculated sum necessary to rectify the damage that has been caused.'

'Have I not the right of protest?' Denham demanded angrily.

'No. Notice of appeal is not permitted in a case of this kind. You may consider yourself fortunate to have escaped personal punishment. The deaths of thousands of people in the United States could very easily have indicted you for manslaughter. That this isn't so is entirely owing to the adroitness of your defending counsel.' The judge paused and then added: 'You have ten days to pay the required reparation to this court, and the dismantling of your various climatic machines will commence as soon as expedient.'

'Dismantle those machines and there will be worldwide disaster!' Denham cried. 'One relies on the other, and if you get one machine stopped and the others still working there will be a catastrophe.'

'All machines can be stopped simultaneously. That is all, Marcus Denham. You are dismissed.'

Bitter, consumed with fury, Denham left the court. He returned to London by air, and it was as he traveled that he thought a good deal. By the time he had returned to the city an idea was clear in his mind. He wasted no time in summoning a meeting of the board of directors of Climate Incorporated, and in silence these gentlemen listened to Denham's story of what had happened in the international court.

'Which means the end of everything,' one of the directors said gloomily. 'One can't defy the international court: it's too powerful.'

'One can — and will,' Denham declared, his small blue eyes bright.

'How?' Richards asked, glancing up.

'Gentlemen,' Denham proceeded grimly, 'the time has come for definite action. We have in our hands an instrument of infinite power by which we can enforce our wishes if we choose. For that very reason, and also because billions are sunk in this project of Climate Incorporated, we are going to take a stand. We're going to stop the court taking away our machines, and we're not going to pay a single cent of that twenty billion dollars claim.'

One of the men grimaced. 'Just words, Denham! They'll not get us very far.'

'Suppose you hear me out before you decide? If we allow the court to get away with this, it means the end of everything. It may also have grave repercussions on the world in general if those machines are dismantled haphazard: that's one good reason why we've got to stand firm. But the main reason is ourselves. We have dictatorship in our hands, and I refuse to believe that any of you won't take advantage of it when you have the chance. In fact, you've got to, or accept ruin.'

'That's true enough,' Richards confirmed. 'But what do you suggest?'

'I suggest warning the countries who have our machines that, if they are interfered with, the country concerned will be held responsible, and reprisal will be exacted. Which it will, with everything we've got.'

'You mean . . . ' Richards seemed to be thinking.

'I mean that what happened to Nicholas Sutherland proves we can govern conditions over a very limited area. A country's capital city, or the entire country itself, can be dealt with just as easily.' Denham went on slowly: 'We can enforce any desired conditions on any country at any time. With such a power as that, we have no need to be at the dictates of any international court — and we're not going to be.'

'What do you mean about Sutherland?' one of the men asked, puzzled.

'Sutherland was a danger to us at one time. Because of that, I had Richards create a violent storm in the area of

Sutherland's home. He was killed in consequence . . . We have too big a thing to let go, gentlemen, and accept consequent ruin. If I have your acquiescence, I will retain Climate Incorporated and build us up into something bigger than that already existing. Nobody exists who can stop us . . . Now, I require a vote of confidence. Does anybody second my proposal to handle this matter exactly as I see fit?'

'I second it,' Richards said promptly.

'Good. We'll take a hand vote. All those in favor?'

Every hand went up, at which Denham smiled. 'You won't regret it, gentlemen. Sooner or later every country has to learn that a new power has risen in the midst — the power of Climate Incorporated. Now let us get down to essentials. By press, radio and television I will warn the countries concerned of reprisal if they dare connive with the international court. I will also issue a warning that any attempt to interfere with the working of London-control will have dire consequences for all concerned.'

'Just one thing,' one of the men said. 'Suppose — as will probably happen — one of the countries refuses to heed your warning? What then? If they go ahead and dismantle a machine, what will happen?'

'Nothing that can't be taken care of,' Richards answered. 'The stoppage of one machine and not the others will cause a certain amount of trouble, but we've learned by now how to get things under control again very rapidly.'

'That being settled,' Denham said, rising, 'I'm bringing this meeting to a close, and I'll get busy right away. There's no time to be lost.'

★　★　★

So Marcus Denham took the step that he knew could only lead to absolute authority. For a time, most nations were stunned by his audacity, and the international court was particularly outraged — but even so, none had the courage to defy Denham's threats. No country was prepared to risk killer-tornadoes or crippling frosts, which were Denham's main threats, for the sake of obeying the international court, so Denham had his way. As indeed he did in London. The military arrived to take charge of the London-control and Denham gave them an hour to get out. If they did not do so, he was determined to shatter the International Court building itself, to say nothing of the town in which it stood, with a terrific magnetic storm . . . The military retired, on orders from the court.

Denham was having his way, and even he was surprised how infinitely powerful was his weapon. And this was only the beginning. Realizing he was virtually unchallengeable, he began to demand this and that, with threats of destruction if he did not get it. By this means he increased his power enormously. No country was particularly to blame for obeying his wishes. How could one defy an organization that at will, could produce the means of crippling a city or a country's entire resources. Denham fought his battle with the threats of fog, crippling frost, and heavy floods — and rather than face such crippling tactics the countries concerned gave in to the demands made upon them. This obtained with the smaller countries, anyhow: the bigger ones began to get together to decide how to deal with this dictator with the winds in his fists.

Russia, the United States and Australia combined their forces in opposition to Climate Incorporated — Australia because she had a climatic machine on her territory; America in revenge for the devastation which had been wrought upon her; and Russia because she had never particularly liked the idea of controlled climate anyhow.

Australia tried first to be rid of the machine within her own borders, but the controllers of the particular station were too quick for her. News of the attempted sabotage was radioed to London-control, and as a consequence Australia — on the verge of spring — suffered the worst long spell of frost in its history. In consequence its cattle were practically all destroyed, and other markets dependent on cattle — wool for instance — were almost wiped out of existence. Added to this was the effect of the six weeks' freezing weather on traffic and movement generally. Australia was virtually paralyzed, and only began to return to normal when she disassociated herself from all further rebellious movements against Climate Incorporated . . . So matters were left to America and Russia.

It was odd, perhaps, but they pooled their military resources to tackle the problem — with disastrous results. Denham was warned of what was coming with the result that dense fog descended on the American and Russian continents, together with strange but violent electrical storms. The outcome of this was inevitable. No planes could fly with their electrical equipment, already affected by polar magnetism, rendered even less trustworthy by deliberately aimed magnetic storms; and no missiles could be fired because the magnetic hazards were too great for the guiding instruments to be trusted. All assurance of accuracy had gone . . . And the fog was the finishing touch. Movement was paralyzed. In both continents it was impossible to see beyond a yard ahead. To launch airplanes, to move armies or ships, was quite impossible — and all supply lines were also reduced to a standstill, unable even to trust their instruments, which normally might have led them through the pall.

And Denham kept his finger on the button, so to speak, until both countries gave him a guarantee of no further attempted hostility. Only then did the iron grip relax with both Russia and America painfully aware of the mighty weapon Denham had in his hands.

Denham smiled to himself, and so did his board of directors. Climate Incorporated was making the world eat out of its hand, and in a rather odd way any war of any kind was rendered impossible. Denham agents maintained a constant surveillance making his grip on the world unique. No gangster ever exacted such toll from his victims. Wealth, commerce, finance — they all flowed to England which was, in a sense, under the dictates of Climate Incorporated. Marcus Denham was established and supremely satisfied that nobody could question his authority, and nobody did . . . for ten years.

By this time the world had come to accept Marcus Denham and Climate Incorporated as a necessary evil. Every country was in his grip, not perhaps visibly since every country still had its own laws and form of society but since climate is the governing factor in any form of existence, Denham naturally had the last word. Rich, immeasurably powerful, he still held the wind in his fists — and Britain, once a rain-sodden island had become a tropical paradise, the edifice of Climate Incorporated being surrounded by giant conifers and palm trees.

The people, too, changed in ten years. The apathy, that had set in when the climate had first started to be controlled, was now complete. The average Englishman or woman was an easy-going, dark-skinned individual of the Spanish type, accustomed now to a warm, genial climate, and, of course, a part of the enormous wealth which had made the country the richest on Earth.

Richards was still scientific chief of the weather, and it was mainly due to his efforts that the compasses and electrical equipment of ships and aircraft were now completely reliable. He had devised a means of insulation, by which magnetic interference was set at zero — so the electrical upheavals generated both by the Poles and the climatic machines no longer caused trouble.

The safety-valve areas in Arctic and Antarctic still existed, and had turned those formerly frigid continents into wastes of rain and hurricane all the year round. Denham had had the brilliant idea of erecting criminal penitentiaries in these regions, an idea to which most countries had agreed. Thereby, convicted criminals were removed from the heart of normal society and transferred to lands of incessant tempest where the residue of normal atmospheric currents raged unceasingly, and indeed essentially. If ever those safety valves ceased to provide outlet, the havoc would be beyond imagining.

Probably in the whole of the world there was nobody who knew that Marcus Denham was cashing in magnificently on an invention which was not his own. The ones who did know, in his immediate circle, were too comfortable to bother — and outside the circle there was Dora Lester, too busy with her own family to be able to do anything. But there was David Brook, now 22 years old — and he of all the people who knew the truth had not forgotten. Though he had not spoken to his Aunt Dora of the strange disappearance of his mother and father, it was never out of his mind. And as he grew older he became more determined to do something about it. Until finally at 22 it was an obsession. He was determined to pit himself against Denham and his climatic machines, and somehow bring him to ruin if that were possible.

No small task! The world was Denham's. Most people were satisfied with things as they now were. But not David Brook. He wanted revenge, and he would never rest until he got it.

Through adolescence he had matured a plan, and at 22 he started to put it into effect. He left the care of Aunt Dora and started out to make his own way — first enlisting in the London Air Force Patrol, an organization specially created by Denham for the purpose of keeping a night and day check on the climatic machines in every country where they were situated.

As Richard Morton, David Brook did his job faithfully and turned in his reports as requested. He was a model pilot, a good engineer, and extremely close-lipped about everything he did. Though he was extremely incommunicative — with good reason considering how much he had on his mind — his fellow pilots liked him, and so did the officials of the organization for which he worked. Great things were promised for the tall, keen-eyed young man — surprisingly unlike his mother and father — who daily did his job of surveying the huge buildings that housed the machines his father had invented.

David never sought company. He spent his off time wandering about alone. He was always thinking, thinking of what he had seen and the plan he had in mind. It was a definite plan, too. Once he had the exact location of every climatic machine — which locations he was gradually pinpointing, thanks to his job of air surveillance — he intended nothing less than the destruction of every machine, no matter what the consequences.

A crazy dream? No. He had access to atomic explosives when he needed them. It would not be difficult either to secure a bomb-carrying plane, and in his spare time he was learning all the details of a bombardier. By the time he was ready for action he intended to gamble everything and thus in some measure avenge his father and mother . . .

He had been in the air force patrol for a year when he came into contact with Ruth Dornsey, a slim gray-eyed blonde employed as a senior clerk in the offices of London-control. The meeting was by chance at an air force patrol social evening but as he came to know Ruth Dornsey better it seemed to David that the occurrence had decided significance. For one thing, Ruth Dornsey, by reason of her job, knew all the details of the various climatic stations. She knew where radiation was emanated from into the upper atmosphere; she knew the positions of the cables that supplied the power to the climatic machine power houses. She knew every detail about them, and technically, was sworn to secrecy concerning them, even though she could not see the reason for it. Her young and innocent mind couldn't possibly see things as Denham saw them — always alert for spies and possible sabotage.

Once he knew secrecy intervened, David set to work to break it down. The girl could help his plans a lot by divulging certain facts. So he went out of his way to win her friendship, and what had begun as a purely business enterprise on David's part, changed gradually to the realization that he was very much in love with Ruth Dornsey. She seemed to have a profound understanding of his nature. Her ideas agreed with his, or at any rate she was clever enough to make them do so. She was in love, too, but so far had not admitted the fact.

'I suppose,' David said, one day when they both had simultaneous off-time and had taken a picnic together, 'you're wondering what kind of a fellow I really am.'

'Not particularly.' Ruth was lying on her back, looking at the cobalt blue of the man-made sky. 'Isn't it enough that I like to be with you? I'd never have come out with you so many times otherwise.'

'But you know so little about me,' David muttered. 'Never have been one to talk much about myself — and yet, in spite of that, you've always come with me when I've asked you . . . Don't you ever wonder who I am? What I am? Why I've so little to say?'

Ruth sat up, the sunlight in her fair hair. No, Dick, I don't really wonder. I've formed my own opinion of your character, and I'm satisfied with it. There can't be anything particularly wrong with your history or you wouldn't be permitted in the Air Force patrol.'

David thought for a moment, then he said: 'There's one deception which I'm going to put straight right away. I rely on you to keep it to yourself. My name isn't really Richard Morton: it's David Brook.'

'One name is as good as another, isn't it?'

'Usually, but in this case I have the

same name as the man who invented control of the weather.'

'Then — ' Ruth looked puzzled. 'Oughtn't your name to be Denham in that case?'

'No. It ought to be Brook, and it is Brook. My father was Alvin Brook, and it was he who invented climatic control.'

'But I've always thought it was Marcus Denham's idea.'

David smiled grimly. 'So does everybody else. I was a child when my father invented it. I remember him demonstrating it to me — and my mother — on a wet summer evening. He took it to Denham to get financial backing. After that my father and mother disappeared and have never been seen since.'

Ruth was silent for a long time, her gray eyes searching David's face. Then at last she nodded slowly.

'Yes, David, I believe you. Every word. Go on.'

'I believe,' David said slowly, 'that they were murdered. How or when this was done I can't say — nor can anybody, apparently — but that's my belief.

Denham cashed in on the idea my father invented and, as you know yourself, control of the climate has given him power such as no man ever possessed before.'

'Yes, that's true enough,' Ruth admitted quietly. 'But what can you do about it? You can't fight Climate Incorporated: it's too powerful.'

'I can — and I'm going to. It's my one object in life. That's why I said you know so little about me. You know now what I'm driving at. I'm going to try to smash Denham and climatic control as well, if it's at all possible. Don't you understand? I owe that much to my father and mother. I'm sure they agree with my obsession, wherever they are.'

'But, David, let's look at this business seriously.' Ruth caught hold of David's hand and looked at him seriously. 'I know how you feel, how you must be consumed with the desire to exact revenge for what's happened — but think for a moment. What chance do you stand? I don't want you to do things that will result in your being killed. You're much too precious to me for that.'

David's hard, frustrated expression passed for a moment. He leaned forward and kissed the girl gently. She kissed him back and for a moment they clung in the embrace of each other; then David tautened again.

'It's not such an impossible thing as it looks,' he said. 'I know the risk, but I'm prepared to take it. I've got to do it, Ruth: it's a sort of duty. Even the fact that I love you, that I may cause you anxiety by following out the plan I've devised, doesn't alter it.'

'All right.' Ruth gave a little shrug. 'You're set on it, and you must do it. All I can do is help you, since I can't dissuade you. I don't agree with Denham's world power any more than you do, but I certainly can't see what I can do about it.'

'You can do a lot. I realized that the moment I knew you were in the offices of London-control . . . ' Then as the girl's face clouded ever so slightly, David added quickly: 'But please don't think that was why I kept so friendly with you. It wasn't. I want you for yourself — more than I've ever wanted anything before.'

Ruth smiled, something of the smile of a mother for a lovable but rather naughty boy. She said:

'I said before that I believe you, and nothing you've said has changed my view . . . So you believe I can help you? Tell me how.'

'Well, for one thing, you know all about the various climatic stations: you know from which point the radiation is emitted into the upper atmosphere; you know the positions of the cables which supply power to the climatic stations. You can even get hold of blueprints setting out in detail all those particulars.'

'Yes, but . . . ' Ruth hesitated; then her gray eyes opened wide. 'Do you realize what you're asking, David? That sort of information is strictly secret. When I joined the staff I was sworn to secrecy on penalty of imprisonment. Everything about climatic control is a closed book to the outer world.'

'I know, but do you know the details I've just mentioned?'

'Certainly. Even so, I can't . . . '

David relaxed a little. He had been

sitting with an arm about Ruth's slim shoulders. Now he suddenly withdrew and sat thinking. He snatched at a piece of grass and twisted it in his fingers.

'It's wrong to drag you into it,' he said finally. 'That shouldn't have to be. You've no axe to grind like I have, and I've no right to ask you to walk into danger to satisfy my wishes . . . Forget it, Ruth.'

'You tell me to forget it after telling me so much! I can't do that, David . . . Tell me how my knowing all the details can help you.'

'All right. In my job as a patrol pilot I view the climatic machine stations constantly from the air, wherever they're situated in every part of the world. I've taken sneak photographs of each one, but it's not easy at the height I am forced to maintain by regulations, to see the details I want. I know the situations of the stations, but I don't know their lifelines, so to speak. For instance, blowing up one of the stations with a bomb would be no use if I didn't succeed in destroying the vital output point. Or, similarly, I might not cut off the power supply. So long as those two points remained undamaged, the engineers could get things rectified in a few short hours. I've got to have absolute destruction when I start.'

Ruth was looking startled, as well she might. 'You don't mean you're going to bomb the climatic stations, surely?'

'Yes.' David nodded almost casually. 'That's just what I'm going to do. Bomb them one after the other. I can get the bombs without much difficulty, and the plane to carry them. And at the speed that plane travels I can complete a circuit of every station and have done the damage before there's hardly time to raise the alarm. However, there's a 'but', and a big one. Which is where you come in.'

'Well?'

'The bombs will be small nuclear ones, but I know Denham's taken the precaution to have the climatic houses shielded against nuclear attack. That means that even a direct hit might be deflected, and I can't afford to miss. I must hit the vital part, either the output or input power. That's why I want the details of where these two vital points are. Once I have that, I can pin-point it on my photographs, and my bombardier training will do the rest.'

Ruth was silent, looking absently in front of her. It was a little time before she stirred herself to speak.

'I can, of course, get the information you want, David — and I know you won't betray my confidence in any way, but do you think it's worth it? You can't get away with destroying the stations. You'll be caught, and you know the penalty.'

'I don't think I shall. I've got it organized. Besides, when the stations are destroyed there'll be such terrible confusion while the climate returns to normal that it will be next to impossible to do anything. Matter of fact, that's the one thing that worries me — the upheaval when the control is gone.'

'You are sure there'll be one?'

'Bound to be. One can't keep natural forces at bay, then suddenly relax the dam, so to speak, without something happening. However, when it's over, things will be back on a normal footing and natural climate will return.'

'Which, as far as England is concerned, won't be too pleasant,' Ruth sighed, with a wistful glance toward the sub-tropical sky.

David got to his feet suddenly and looked down at the girl, his face grim. 'Listen, Ruth, this matter goes far beyond fine weather considerations. I like tropical England as much as anybody, but I'm trying to take the realistic view — namely, that my mother and father were murdered by Marcus Denham, and that the whole world has to bow to this money-grubbing dictator because he's using a stolen secret. Nobody else is going to do anything, so I'm going to — yes, even if it kills me.'

'Nobody else?' Ruth questioned. 'I'm going to do my share, or had you forgotten?'

'Sorry . . . ' David looked at her for a moment. 'I got carried away for the moment.'

'I know, dearest . . . But what you're going to do is right as far as you know it to be, and for that reason I'm with you.

I'll get those particulars you want the moment I return to work. Then you can work it out. That right?'

'Perfect.' David smiled, and kissed the girl warmly as she raised her face to his — then again they settled own in the grass, talking, soaking in the blazing heat of the summer sun. They only moved when hunger would no longer be denied, going hand in hand through the tall, dry grass in the direction of the little village close by.

They had vanished from sight when a third person rose out of the grass — a shabbily clothed individual with three days of stubble on his weather-beaten face and hair so long it reached down into the collar of his threadbare jacket. Definitely one of nature's gentlemen if ever there was one. Hobos were few in these days, but those who did take to the road were sure of reliable weather. So it was with Horace Alfred Jenkins, ex-actor, tramping the country for reasons of both health and finance. But now he saw a chance to perhaps relieve his monetary embarrassment. The words David and

Ruth had exchanged would make inter-esting hearing to Marcus Denham.

Horace Alfred Jenkins went on his way through the grass, his destination London, looming on the near horizon in all its ultra modern might . . .

7

Arctic Penitentiary

To secure an interview with Marcus Denham was difficult at the best of times, and for a down-at-heel tramp like Jenkins it was nearly impossible. Then mention of the name David Brook, by way of the commissionaire, seemed to do the trick. Horace Alfred Jenkins got his interview.

'Well?' Denham demanded, impaling Jenkins with a fierce blue eye. 'What's all this nonsense you've been talking about David Brook?'

'It is not nonsense, my good sir: it is truth.' Jenkins spoke in his best actor's voice and spread his hands at the same time. 'All this afternoon I lay in the grass and listened to David Brook talking to a young girl by the name of Ruth.'

'Well, what's so unique about that, man? Young men and young women have been talking nonsense to each other ever since the world began.'

'True, sir, but this was not nonsense. They talked of nothing else but the destruction of climatic control, and the murder of David Brook's mother and father.'

'Oh?' Denham concealed his surprise. He motioned to a chair but Jenkins shook his head.

'No, sir, I think not. My clothes are not in the best of condition for such furniture as this office possesses. I will remain standing, with your permission . . . All I require is some slight financial token of gratitude in return for what I have to tell you.'

'I don't bargain with vagrants!' Denham snapped, at which Jenkins shrugged.

'So be it, sir. In that case I will be on my way — '

'Not until you've opened your mouth you won't. Come, man — what did those two discuss?'

'It is worth a financial reward,' Jenkins insisted.

'You won't go away empty-handed: you have my word on that. Now start talking.'

Jenkins hesitated; then he obeyed. He repeated in detail the conversation David and Ruth had had, right from the moment when David had said: 'I suppose you're wondering what kind of a fellow I am?'

At the end of the repetition Denham sat meditating, an unlit cigar speared between his teeth.

'Very interesting,' he commented finally. 'Very interesting indeed. I'm quite indebted to you, Mr. Jenkins.'

'I thought you would be, sir. That being so, may I ask for financial return for the information?'

'You may ask,' Denham shrugged, 'but you won't get it. It is quite obvious that you've heard a good many things concerning me things that I should not like repeated in public. I have to safeguard myself, you understand?'

'Rest assured, sir, that not a word will escape me.'

'I intend to be absolutely sure of that.' Denham pressed a button on his desk and after a considerable interval the commissionaire from the entrance hall entered.

'Yes, Mr. Denham?'

'Mr. Jenkins is leaving. See that he is conducted properly out of the building.'

'Look here — ' Jenkins started to protest, but he had no chance to get any further. He was whirled out into the corridor and the office door closed. Immediately Denham reached to the telephone and rang a number swiftly.

'London-control, clerical division,' came a voice in the receiver.

'Denham here. Check up among your senior officials in the clerical division and see if you have a young woman by the name of Ruth working among you. I want her surname.'

'Right, sir. I'll call you back.'

Denham grunted something and rang off. Then he contacted, again by phone, the air force patrol headquarters and was soon in touch with the personnel officer.

'I believe,' Denham said, 'you have a young pilot on the patrol list by the name of Richard Morton. Will you check on that and give me the particulars of his background, history and so forth?'

'It won't take a moment, sir.'

There was an interval, during which Denham sat doodling on his blotter and listening to the rustle of papers at the other end. Then the voice spoke again:

'Richard Morton, sir, is aged 22 and joined the patrol a year ago. A first-class pilot and has done his work well. His background is rather hazy. Apparently an orphan, brought up by an aunt. Nothing much more about him . . . Height about five-foot-ten, blue-eyed and brown-haired.'

'Right. Now listen: Remove Morton from all patrols until further instructions from me. Ground him. Do not give him access to anything of a secret nature. Understood?'

'I'll do exactly as you order, sir.'

Denham rang off and scowled in thought for a moment, then as the phone shrilled he whipped it up.

'Yes? Denham here.'

'Clerical division, sir. We have an employee in the senior department by the name of Ruth Dornsey. She is the only Ruth on the list, so probably she's the person about whom you were asking.'

'Thank you,' Denham said curtly, and

rang off. In another moment he was in contact with the central police division. The voice of the police chief himself answered.

'I've a job for you,' Denham said. 'And I want it done properly. Investigate the life and background of pilot Richard Morton of the air force patrol. His real name is probably David Brook. Let me know what information you get, and I want it quickly . . . Also take precautions against him making any attempt to obtain bombs or explosive by false pretences. Advise the necessary quarters. Check?'

'I'll attend to it, Mr. Denham.'

'There's another thing. I want you to find the home address of Ruth Dornsey, a young woman in the clerical division of C.I. Have her picked up and brought to me.'

'As soon as possible,' the chief agreed.

Denham rang off and then glanced up as the hall commissionaire entered.

'I dispatched Jenkins as you requested, sir,' he announced.

'Good. Where did you send him?'

'At the moment, sir, he's on his way to

the Antarctic penitentiary. I assumed that would be in order.'

'Quite in order,' Denham grinned. 'If he'd been left to his own devices he could have been quite a nuisance . . . All right, you can go.'

The door closed. Denham got to his feet, stubbed his cigar in the ashtray, and then crossed to the window. Grim-faced, he looked out onto the calm of the summer evening spread over the city.

'Evidently providence is watching over me,' he muttered. 'But for that tramp young Brook might have got away with it. Damned if I hadn't forgotten that Alvin Brook's son existed.'

The one thing Denham wanted was action there and then — but it was impossible to get it. The police had to make the investigations that had been ordered — as far as David was concerned — and Ruth Dornsey had to be traced and picked up. Tracing her was not difficult, but the picking up did not happen until that night after she had left David. The time being then inconvenient to Denham he gave orders for the girl to be held until he was ready for her, as the worried Ruth was transferred to the city prison to await developments. She had a good idea what these developments would be, but for the life of her she could not understand how information had leaked out. Surely nobody could have overheard anything, out in the expanse of open fields?

It was two days before Denham got the information he wanted. He had David Brook picked up and, along with Ruth Dornsey, he was brought to Denham's office. In silence he watched them brought in, then he dismissed the police officers and sat regarding the two young people facing him.

'Naturally, you're wondering what all this is about?' he asked grimly, his eyes fixed on David's grim, unyielding face. 'I'll tell you right away . . . It concerns a conversation you two had together in the fields a couple of days ago.'

'I didn't know you had spies there, too,' David retorted. 'I know that the city and its environs is riddled with Denham agents, but evidently your snooping extends further than that.'

'It won't pay you to adopt that tone, Brook,' Denham said coldly. 'I know exactly who you are, thanks to police inquiry, and I also know what you intended to do to the various climatic machines in different parts of the world . . . A very foolhardy plan, if I may say so — and there's even more shame on you for dragging this girl into it, too.'

'I came into it of my own accord,' Ruth said, her face defiant. 'No force was used. After what David told me, I quite agreed with his plans.'

Denham shrugged. 'More fool you, young woman. You are trying to help a young man who is obviously mad. I suppose he's told you of his crazy dream of overthrowing Climate Incorporated, under the delusion that it was his own father who invented weather control? In fact I *know* he has told you.'

'It is the truth,' David snapped. 'You murdered my father and mother in some way or other, and stole the invention my father tried to sell to you!'

Denham sighed. 'All right, I won't

argue with you. The only thing that surprises me is that the air force patrol ever passed you as mentally and physically sound. However, the truth has been discovered in time.'

Denham reflected for a moment, his small blue eyes on David's face. 'I take it you have heard of the Arctic and Antarctic penitentiary areas?'

Ruth gave a start and looked at David quickly, then she looked back at Denham.

'You're not going to send him there, surely? You can't! You just — '

'Don't presume to tell me what I can do, Miss Dornsey! You evidently don't realize how dangerous a man David Brook — or Richard Morton — really is. Mentally unbalanced in one direction, but sane enough in others. Not unbalanced enough to need incarceration in one of our mental institutions, but dangerous enough to be a criminal. What you have plotted, Brook, amounts to high treason.'

'And I'll carry it out before I'm finished,' David retorted. 'You can imprison me, give me solitary confinement if you wish, but I'll still come back.'

'You talk like the madman you are,' Denham commented. 'Remember this: if I chose I can have you put to death for treason, which is the normal penalty for such a crime, but I prefer to let you think about the crime you've tried to perpetrate, and there is no better place for a man to think than in the Arctic penitentiary! You will never come back from there, my deluded friend.'

David did not answer. He had partly been expecting such a sentence. His main worry was not for himself, but for Ruth. He was bitterly conscious of how he had dragged her into his scheme.

'As for you, young woman . . . ' Denham's hard eyes moved to the girl. 'As for you, your employment in the clerical division of this organization will end forthwith. You will be transferred to the women's labor corps for a period of three years, which naturally means you will be divested of all civic rights.'

'Why turn the girl into a criminal for something which I attempted to do?' David demanded. 'She was an innocent party, only doing as I asked.'

'Of her own free will,' Denham retorted. 'Don't presume to tell me what to do, Brook. You've heard my decision and that's the end of it.'

He pressed a button on his desk and two uniformed police officials, obviously planted in an anteroom beforehand, came into the office.

'Take them out,' Denham ordered. 'You know what you have to do.'

Ruth made an attempt to speak but was promptly silenced and bundled outside. David was not so easily handled; he tore free of the grip upon him and swung round to Denham.

'I'm warning you, Denham — I'll come back. No matter what you do. You're not going to get away with it forever. You — '

David did not get the chance to say any more. He was seized again, more firmly this time, and forced out into the corridor. Ahead of him, down the long vista, Ruth was fighting and shoving helplessly in the grip of the official who had charge of her.

'Courage, Ruth!' David yelled after her.

'I'll come back for you before I'm — '
then he broke off as a vicious slap was
delivered across his face. Ahead of him
Ruth was whirled round a corner and
disappeared.

★　★　★

From then on, David Brook's life was a
nightmare. He was kept in the city for
two days and nights, in the prison cells,
and then was transferred to the latest
batch of criminals due for the Arctic
penitentiary. Hardened cases, most of
them, and the guards not much better.
A special airplane, of the troop-carrying
variety, made the journey from London to
the storm-lashed wastes of the Arctic, in
the midst of which loomed a solitary
plateau where stood the forbidding edifice
of Arctic penitentiary.

Once within the walls of this frowning
edifice and David Brook became a part
of the sour-faced, bitter army of men
who were cut off by guards and weather
conditions from all sight and sound of
normal civilization. Here worked and

slept and died the outcasts of society, men who had never returned to the outer world from which they had been sent.

But David Brook never lost heart, even though absorbed into this mire of human misery. He was not dead, and that was the main thing. As long as there was life there was still a chance, and being quite a young man, his physique was equal to the tasks of hard labor thrust upon him.

Altogether, he was a model prisoner. He gave the guards no trouble, incited no riots, and made no demands. Each day he worked immensely hard, usually digging rock and rubble in lashing rain and screaming wind, helping to lay the foundations of an extension to the penitentiary.

But all the time he watched his chance, or thought of the climatic machines, or perhaps Ruth. What had happened to her, and was she now absorbed in the labor corps? If anything made him anxious to escape it was the thought of Ruth, or the sneering satisfaction of Denham. Denham, the man responsible for all this! Denham, the murderer, the thief . . .

David went on digging, an iron-muscled, grim-faced young man. He made friends of sorts, men who like him had been outlawed for some offence against the laws instituted by Denham. One friend in particular — Martin Fornham — shared his cell with him. He was a man of 45, aged 20 years beyond his time by the endless toiling amidst nearly impossible climatic conditions.

David and Martin Fornham came at last to an exchange of confidences, after eight months of captivity together. Each felt he could trust the other, and it was quite clear from Fornham's conversation that he was convinced the Arctic penitentiary was the end of the line.

'You talk about escaping,' he said, lying on his bunk and eyeing David in the dim cell light. 'There isn't an earthly chance of it, lad. Nothing but tempest and a devil's ocean all around us, and the place crawling with guards. No living soul can beat that — and even if you got as far as the ocean, you'd be shot before you could cover a dozen yards.'

'There's a supply plane once a month,'

David remarked. 'I'm a skilled pilot. I might arrange somehow to steal that plane.'

'A fool's idea. You'd get nowhere. Once on this plateau and it's the finish. Try to start realizing it.'

'Why should I? I'm young: I've got important things to do, and no infernal penitentiary is going to stop me. I'll get out — somehow.'

'Up to you,' Fornham shrugged. 'I've tried it, and I know it can't be done. Besides, things have been tightened up since I made my attempt . . . Anyway, what are you so anxious to get out for? Got a wife or sweetheart waiting for you?'

'I have a girl, yes. In the labor corps for trying to help me. She got landed there and I came here.'

'What was the charge?'

'Marcus Denham called it treason . . . I planned nothing less than the destruction of his climatic machines. They're ruination. He's got world dictatorship because he owns them.'

Fornham meditated, drawing on the meager ration of his cigarette. 'I suppose,' he said, 'that most men will cash in to the utmost on an invention which will give them power. Denham's doing no more than that. Unfortunately, he happens to be a pretty bad lot.'

'More than that — he's a murderer. My father was the real inventor of climatic control. He died at Denham's hands, and so did my mother. I'd planned everything so that I could smash the climatic machines in revenge but things went wrong. So — I'm here.'

'Your father was the real inventor?' Fornham repeated incredulously.

'Yes.' David gave the details as he lay propped on one elbow in his bunk. 'Now you can see why I want revenge.'

'Sure I can see — but I think you went the wrong way about it. You don't need to smash the climatic machines to destroy weather control. There's an easier way, if you can do it. I ought to know. I used to be a Met man, but with the coming of climatic control I fell on hard times, did some thieving and generally got into trouble, and ended up here.'

'What do you mean — there's an easier

way?' David demanded.

'Simple enough.' Fornham crushed out his cigarette stub on the edge of the bunk. 'Find a way to bottle up the tempest areas, and climatic control will soon finish. Or, more correctly, it will blow up. Explode.'

David slid from his bunk and crossed to the older man. He looked down on him with fixed interest.

'Explode? What are you talking about?'

'Look, lad, how do you think climatic control stands up? How do you think it functions?'

'By hot and cold currents produced by molecular vibration. I know that from what my father told me from time to time, and I've had time during the years to read his notes, which my Aunt found in our old home.'

'Then you ought to know that there have to be safety areas, as they're called. Of recent years the 'safety-valve' areas have been located in the Arctic and Antarctic: that's why the weather here is in a constant turmoil. The vibratory currents issued from the climatic stations form a barrier to normal atmospheric conditions, and don't allow those normal conditions to operate. They have to be discharged somewhere — just the same as steam in a boiler would blow up the boiler if it hadn't a safety-valve.'

'So the Arctic and Antarctic regions are really the normal air currents discharging themselves — the currents that normally would flow over the world?' David questioned.

'That's it. Warmth, cold, rain, wind — they all discharge at the Poles, which creates the tempest spots.'

David sat in thought on the edge of Fornham's bunk. Fomham looked at him for a moment or two and then added:

'So you see — destroying the climatic machines is only one way. There's the other way — bottling up the safety valves. Since one is as impossible as the other, it's not worth worrying over.'

'Perhaps not so impossible,' David said slowly, looking into space. 'Perhaps not, Mart.'

'No? For instance?'

'Suppose a climatic machine the same

as the others in the world were to be built and operated in this penitentiary? Suppose there was another like it in the Antarctic pen?'

Fornham stared. 'But it's impossible, lad!'

'Suppose it were to be done? What would happen with the twin polar tempest areas controlled separately from the rest of the climate?'

'The control would have nothing to do with it. The point would be that the safety-valve system would cease to function. There wouldn't be anywhere in the world for the normal currents to escape.'

David smiled. 'Exactly . . . ' He clenched his fists. 'Mart, you've given me something to work on. Something to live for. An objective, and situated right here under my nose. Somehow we've got to have climatic machines at the poles, secretly, working in opposition to the normal machines and preventing the tempest areas from working. Before they're found out, we hope, there'll be an upheaval of some kind and the normal winds and currents will smash through the barrier, bringing an end to climatic control — and Marcus Denham.'

'And who the devil do you think is going to listen to a cockeyed scheme like that?'

'I don't know — offhand. But I'll find out. The idea's there: it only wants developing.'

And upon that David drifted over slowly to his bunk again — but he hardly slept that night. His head was too full of schemes . . .

★ ★ ★

Thereafter, David did not waste any time in going into action, starting first by testing a theory which he had held privately ever since he had become a prisoner on the Arctic plateau. He knew he was risking everything but he considered it worth it. He could not be in a much worse position than he was at present, and the chance he was going to take might lead to freedom.

The next day, when his shift of work was over, he succeeded in being granted an interview with the prisoner governor, a hard-faced, grim-eyed man, no happier than the prisoners he controlled. There was talk of the fact that he was a criminal himself, otherwise he would never have been on this tempest-lashed plateau surrounded by dangerous men and merciless gray walls.

'Well, what do you want?' he asked curtly, as David faced him across the desk. 'Make it short.'

David said quietly, 'Are you prepared to talk to me as man to man for a moment, and not as a prison governor? I've something important to tell you, and you know from my record that I'm a model prisoner. How about giving me a chance?'

'All right, but don't take too long. I've a lot to do.'

'What would you be prepared to do to get away from this island, this storm-bound plateau?' David asked deliberately; and the governor's eyebrows rose in surprise.

'What would I be prepared to do?' he repeated, then he laughed shortly. 'Got the cart before the horse, haven't you? A governor has no wish to escape: it's the prisoner who wants to do that.'

'I know, and I wish to escape as much as anybody. I'm trying to find out, sir, if you wish to do so as well.'

'I should imagine anybody in their right senses would be glad to get away from here,' the governor shrugged. 'As far as I am concerned, it can't be done. I've duties to perform.'

'The duties of governor,' David said. 'For what? For Marcus Denham, and nobody else. Why don't you look at this thing in the right light? In a place like this you're as much a prisoner as anybody else. All of us doomed to stay on this plateau, at the mercy of the most violent weather conditions ever known to man.'

'We put up with it,' the governor said, musing.

'We've no need to,' David snapped. 'You know some of the facts about me, but I don't think you know the real reason for my being here.'

'The records say treasonable activity.'

'Which is a complete lie. I'm David

Brook by real name, the son of Alvin Brook who invented weather control. Marcus Denham has no legal right to control of the weather.'

'Oh?' The Governor waited, his brow raised; then he listened as David gave him the facts. When he had heard them, he gave a whimsical smile.

'Even if I believe you — as I am inclined to do — I don't see what can be done about it. You haven't an earthly chance of proving your case in any court of law. If I thought that was possible I'd grant you leave to enlist legal aid — '

'I don't want it. All I need is your co-operation to smash Marcus Denham completely — and the grip C.I. has on the world. It can be done, right here. The only other thing necessary is collusion with Antarctica penitentiary. Get that, and Marcus Denham will be finished.'

'How will he? If this is just a pipedream, you — '

'It's no pipedream. If we built a climatic machine here, and another in Antarctica, and so bottled up completely the safety valves, climatic control — and

Denham — would end in a fortnight, or even less. I can build such a machine because I know from years of study from my father's original draft plans exactly what he put into the apparatus. I can't make bricks without straw, though. If you can get the materials, I'll do the rest . . . '

The governor was silent, his work forgotten, his eyes looking through the window on to the gale-driven rain outside. After a moment he got to his feet and paced thoughtfully around the office.

'I could have you transferred to solitary for what you've said,' he commented, smiling grimly. 'I should even be within my rights in sentencing you to death — but as I said before, I believe you. I believe you for another reason apart from my being a judge of character — the reason that I, too, was sent here for a crime I did not commit. Everybody here, captives and guards, has supposedly offended against society in some way — or, more accurately, has been a little too obvious in rebelling against Climate Incorporated. I have nothing to lose by giving you a chance, Brook. It doesn't matter to me if every prisoner on this plateau escapes, so long as I escape with them . . . What you're doing is putting the spark to a rebellion. You realize that?'

David nodded. 'Yes. Somebody has to, and I've more reason than anybody, particularly after what happened to my father and mother. I'll carry this thing through to the end, or die in the attempt. Rely on that.'

'I do rely on it, because if there is a mistake all of us will suffer. We'll be exterminated to a man . . . Now, you spoke of collusion with our opposite number Antarctica. Presumably to get them on our side and have a climatic machine similar to ours constructed?'

'Exactly so. I should imagine that the governor and warders of Antarctica feel pretty much as you do: they only need to be talked to, and you're the man to do it. Get them on our side, then we'll discuss further. You have a closed radio circuit to the Antarctic penitentiary, so there's no fear of C.I. hearing what you have to say. In fact, I don't suppose they're even concerned with what's happening in the prisons, so secure do they feel in their sub-tropical paradise.'

'I'll get in touch,' the governor promised. 'Now, what are the materials you want?'

'Electrical equipment, which I'll have to itemize in a detailed list. We'll need a lot of it, and atomic generators as well.'

The governor frowned. 'That won't be easy. There might be an inquiry. I can get most things, but they have to look legitimate.'

'They can this time. An extension is being built to the penitentiary: I ought to know since I've done most of the digging along with my fellow prisoners. Say the electrical stuff is required for the prison extensions: nobody will question that.'

'Yes, I could probably get away with it,' the governor admitted. 'And what about Antarctica? What's their excuse going to be? No extensions are being made there.'

'Have everything sent here. We'll assemble both machines here — which is necessary since I'm the only one who knows how to do it. We'll break the Antarctica machine down into sections and fly the parts there, where any good engineer will be able to assemble them. There shouldn't be any difficulty about that: you have the authority to get freight planes when you want them.'

The governor gave his taut smile. 'Got everything worked out, haven't you?'

'Certainly. I've had a long time to think about it. The whole thing relies on me trusting you, and you trusting me. Since we both of us have been transported here for something we didn't do we ought to make good partners — and in ridding the world of Marcus Denham we'll be even more than that; we'll be benefactors.'

'True enough . . . ' the governor reflected for a moment. 'There's another side — the long view. When climatic control can't function anymore what's going to happen? I know we'll be rid of Denham and his whole organization because if climatic control abruptly ceases the people will turn upon him — but what's going to happen to the world itself? Will there be a cataclysm?'

'Beyond question — but its fury and extent I don't know. We'll survive, as man has always done. Then afterwards we can ... ' David stopped and sighed. 'I just don't know. It'll be a clean slate to work on, I suppose. I know how climatic control *should* be run to make everybody happy. But that's in the future. We've a big job to do first.'

'All right.' The governor made a decisive movement. 'You work out the specifications for materials, and I'll do the rest. Let me know when you're ready.'

8

Atomic reprisal

A year passed, and to England and the countries paying the highest fees, there came again a cloudless summer. America, Canada, and the whole of Western Europe basked in the still, burning glory of a gigantic man-made anti-cyclone, a high pressure system which would remain motionless until the autumn when, at Denham's word, conditions would change to much-needed rain.

And at the Poles of the Earth there were still the tempest-spots, the safety valves by which the normal air currents made their escape. Reports from the prisons at either Pole showed everything to be satisfactory. Not that Denham cared anyway. The outcasts of society, or those dangerous to him, were shut away for good, cut off from those nearest and dearest to them, grinding out what was left of their lives in continents where the sun never shone, and where the temperature varied from frigid to tropical in a matter of hours. Certainly nobody ever suspected that a rebellion had started, and that the cloud no larger than a man's hand was already forming — and through the summer grew in dimensions and importance.

Only one person in particular thought often of the Arctic penitentiary and sighed wistfully for what might have been . . . Ruth Dornsey, with some of her three-year sentence with the women's labor corps behind her. She thought constantly of David and wondered what had happened to him: she even made plans for trying to visit him when her sentence was ended. Otherwise she went on day by day, uniformed, divested of all civilian rights and freedom, working in the clerical section of the corps whose main function was the setting up of communications between cities — electrical and telephone — a task not too heavy for women, but with all the rigidity of prison discipline, just the same.

And in this sunny calmness, scientist Richards was also a power in the land. His complete disavowal of principles and his loyalty to Marcus Denham had made him a wealthy, influential man. He came and went as he pleased, an army of scientists always at his beck and call. He traveled leisurely around the storm-free world, calling at the various climatic stations to survey their functions, lounging in the best hotels with an endless supply of money at his command.

Yet the cloud no bigger than a man's hand grew a little larger, and the first definite sign of its presence came in mid-July when Richards was on one of his usual tours of inspection. He got a decided shock when he visited the colossal edifice at Spitzbergen, which housed the climatic machine nearest to the Arctic Circle. Not that the Arctic Circle as such existed any more: it was, as ever, one of the tempest spots, the fury of insane weather conditions existing a scant 100 miles from the sunny Spitzbergen station.

Yes, Richards got a shock. He stood at

the far end of the huge gangway that ran down the central length of the station. He looked at the great black wall of dials and studied them in silence. They gave reports of the atmospheric pressure in every part of the world, together with a dozen other factors essential to the balanced control of the climate. But there was something different from previous occasions.

Normally, the meters attached to the other stations around the world should be recording a constant '0' — the zero equivalent of non-disturbance. But this time this was not so. There were big divergences between stations, some recording as high as '5' degrees disturbance, and others '2' and '3.'

Turning abruptly, Richards snapped his fingers. The resident boss of the station caught his signal and came hurrying over.

'Why hasn't this been reported to London?' Richards demanded, nodding to the dials. 'You've got one to five degrees of disturbance and never said anything about it.'

'I didn't see any reason to worry London-control.'

'What the hell do you mean — didn't see any reason?'

'The disturbance isn't causing any trouble, Mr. Richards. The machines in all stations are functioning perfectly: we keep a constant check on that.'

'Naturally, that's part of your job, but you're also expected to use your initiative. Can't you see that there's outside influence at work here, which has nothing to do with the smooth running of the stations?'

The station chief looked puzzled. 'But what outside influence can there be? There just isn't any with the whole world ringed with stations.'

'It's there, and we've got to know why,' Richards snapped. He inspected the dials again and then asked: 'How much disturbance value is produced by being so near to the Arctic tempest spot?'

'About two. Never more.'

'Yet here we've got five, and not limited to this one station. There's disturbance on every station, which shows climatic control is no longer in perfect balance. I've got to find out why. What are the barometric readings?'

The chief looked at the instrument. 'Thirty-one. Very slight fall.'

'Fall!' Richards' eyebrows went up. He crossed to the big standard aneroid and tapped it. The needle deflected slightly at the impact.

'And still dropping,' Richards said, grim-faced. 'That just ought not to be. Something's got to be done, and quickly. Get me a detailed report on all these dial readings. I'll take them back to London with me.'

The station chief complied and, within half an hour, Richards was back once more in his plane, frowning to himself as the pilot hurtled the machine through cloudless heaven as fast as the jets could take it.

Once back in London, Richards did not hesitate for a moment. He went direct to C.I. headquarters and laid his information before Denham. Denham listened and then scowled through the reports Richards had brought back with him.

'Doesn't make sense to me,' he said finally. 'How can you get a falling barometer in an anti-cyclone? We've got a high-pressure area clean to the west coast of America on one side, to mid-Europe on the other. The damned barometer must be wrong.'

'Not that one.' Richards bit his lower lip worriedly. 'It's one of the best instruments made. I'll check on it, though.'

He reached to the intercom and switched it on. As a voice responded he said curtly:

'Give me London-control. Chief engineer.'

In another moment the engineer replied: 'Yes, Mr. Denham?'

'This isn't Mr. Denham; it's Richards. Give me your barometric reading, please.'

A pause, then: 'Thirty-one, slight fall.'

'Thanks. How do your climatic-station indicators read?'

'One to five-degree disturbance as one moves northwards.'

'Thanks. Notify any other change.'

Richards switched off and met the grim blue eyes of Denham across the desk. His cigar, projecting from his jaws, had gone out.

'Identical,' Richards said. 'London and Spitzbergen show the same readings. But why, in heaven's name? What's upsetting things?'

'Probably one of the machines isn't functioning properly. That would cause disturbance on instruments, though not enough to be noticed by the eye. Everything looks all right — no clouds, no wind.'

'Yet the high pressure's falling,' Richards insisted, 'and it seems to be falling from the north if the degree of disturbance on the climatic machines is correct . . . As for the machines themselves, they're all right. I've just finished the round trip of checking them.'

'Then what's the answer?'

'Hanged if I know. At the moment it has me beaten. If the pressure goes on falling it might have disastrous consequences.'

Denham lighted his extinguished cigar and looked at the reports again. Richards wandered to the window and gazed steadily down on to the city, his mind trying to find a way around the problem.

He started when, after a moment, Denham suddenly snapped his fingers.

'Richards, I've got an idea . . . '

Richards came over to him. 'Well? Let's have it.'

'Pressure's falling from the north: that's established. Very well, what have we in the north — '

'Only the safety-valve area. I checked on the disturbance that might be expected from that.'

'We have more than the safety-valve area. We have a penitentiary, and in it there's David Brook.'

Richards stared. 'Well? How does David Brook fit in?'

'I don't know exactly, but I'm going to hazard a guess. David Brook is the only living man outside ourselves who knows all about climatic control from his father. It seems too much of a coincidence for mysterious pressure to come from the north and David Brook not to have something to do with it.'

Richards thought for a moment, then he laughed disbelievingly.

'But what on Earth can he have to do

with it, locked up in a penitentiary?'

'I tell you I don't know. I can only say that David Brook is our sworn enemy, and extremely knowledgeable as far as climate control is concerned . . . Let me think for a moment.'

Denham frowned to himself and drew hard on his cigar. After a while he sighed and tightened his lips.

'Don't see there's anything he could do. I should have wiped him out to begin with and been sure. He can't — ' Denham stopped, whipping his cigar from his mouth. 'Say, wait a minute! I've just remembered something. A requisition I had to okay some time ago.'

Richards waited, completely in the dark, as Denham switched on the intercom to his secretary and spoke briefly.

'About a year ago, Miss Bennett, a request was received by us from Arctic penitentiary for some electrical equipment. I remember I had to okay it. Would you turn it up, please, and let me have it right away?'

'Certainly, Mr. Denham.'

Denham switched off and looked at the

puzzled Richards.

'I believe I've got it, Richards, and if I have our troubles can soon be over. It's all my own fault for not disposing of young Brook sooner. I was wrong in my belief that he ought to sweat it out and die from sheer monotony.'

'What's this about electrical equipment? I don't recall anything of that nature.'

'Hardly likely, since I never told you. Electrical stuff was ordered for the prison extensions — '

Denham broke off as the austere Miss Bennett came into the office with a folder. She laid it on the desk. 'There it is, sir. Anything further?'

'No, thanks.'

The woman left. Denham opened the file and studied the contents, then he clapped his hands together in sudden satisfaction.

'Richards, we've got it! The governor of Arctic penitentiary ordered a mass of equipment, and at first sight it looks normal enough, but just read it for yourself. You know as much about building a climatic machine as I do.'

Richards took the file and pored over it. He made one or two calculations and sketches on the desk scratchpad, and then finally he looked up in amazement.

'These requirements are exactly what one would require to build a couple of climatic machines.'

'A couple?' Denham repeated in surprise.

'Certainly. There is two of everything — even two atomic generators.'

'In case of failure of any one part,' Denham said, thinking. 'Yes, that will be it — But you gather the drift now, I suppose?'

'Only too well! Brook's a bright boy — and quite frankly, sir, it surprises me you didn't see it at the time you gave your okay.'

Denham shrugged. 'I'm not apologizing. I'd no reason to suspect anything . . . But I have now. And I think the prison governor himself must be in on it as well. The request was signed by him in the first place.'

Richards gestured with sudden briskness.

'Looks as if we have the answer. Brook has somehow built a climatic machine at the penitentiary and has got it in action. The influence of it is extending over our ordered climatic system and causing a lowering in pressure. That means . . . '

Richards gave a start. 'I've got it! He's trying to seal the safety-valve area at the Arctic!'

'So — it would seem,' Denham muttered.

'That's serious. With only the Antarctic safety-valve there might be a lot of unpleasant repercussions . . . We've got to stop this before things get too awkward.'

Denham grinned viciously. 'We'll stop it all right, never fear.'

'Naturally you'll go over personally and find out what's going on?'

'Not I!' Denham got to his feet and drew hard on his cigar again. 'Do you take me for an idiot, man? For one thing, I don't relish having to fly in that tempest spot, and for another it's possible that the whole prison's in such a state of revolt that I'd be shot down before I could even approach it. No, this calls for something really drastic if we're to keep climatic control and save our own skins.'

'What do you suggest?'

'Nothing less than blowing Arctic pen out of the Earth — destroy the whole building, the inmates, and the secret climatic machine.' Denham clenched his fists. 'Give them no time to argue, no warning — Just drop a couple of nuclear bombs on the pen and that will be the end of that.'

'Definitely,' Richards agreed, rather soberly. 'And future criminals? Where will you send them?'

'Antarctic, of course, or else use the lethal chamber more than we have been doing. That's beside the point. It's this present emergency we have to meet.'

Denham did not hesitate a moment longer. He snatched up the telephone and gave the necessary orders to his Air Patrol Chief; then he put the phone down with a satisfied smile and looked at Richards again.

'That settles that, my friend. You heard my orders? In an hour a fleet will take off, carrying two nuclear bombs ... Keep your eyes on London-control's meters for the next few hours and you'll very soon see things back to normal.'

★ ★ ★

An hour later the air patrol fleet departed in strength, two of the machines carrying a bomb each, and small though they were, each bomb was capable of liquidating a medium-sized city. Denham, seated in his office, and Richards in London-control, both watched the flight through their television screens and what they saw gave them every satisfaction.

As the Arctic penitentiary hove into view, situated on the main Arctic plateau, and lashed by the eternal rain and winds, there was no sign of opposition — or else it was that the inmates realized it was impossible, with their limited resources, to deal with an armed fleet. Whatever the reason, the bombs were dropped according to plan, with all their destructive and far-reaching violence.

When the job was finished there was

nothing but a crater where the penitentiary and extensions had been. Swiftly the fleet turned about and then returned to the London base . . . The job was done and Denham relaxed with satisfaction. David Brook and his machinations had been well and truly dealt with.

Richards, for his part, switched off the televisor and then looked at his watch. An hour had passed since the actual bombing of the pen, so there ought to be a change just starting to register on the various climatic-machine indicators — and also the barometer. He left his office to investigate and presently entered the main power-room of the building.

A shock awaited him as he gazed at the meters connected with the other stations. There was no sign of a return to '0' and normalcy. If anything, there was a slight increase from '5' to '7.'

'It's incredible,' Richards whispered to himself, and crossed quickly to the barometer. In response to the tap he gave it, the needle flickered slightly on the downward scale, giving a drop of nearly a quarter of an inch of pressure.

That was enough for Richards. He left the power-room and went by the shortest route to Denham's headquarters, catching him just as he was about to leave the office for the day.

'It's no different, Mr. Denham!' he exclaimed. 'Pressure is still falling, and the climatic stations show an added disturbance.'

Denham hesitated for a moment before replying, then he shrugged away the scientist's anxiety.

'You haven't given things time enough to settle down, Richards. Then again, the nuclear bombs would make another disturbance. All things considered, it's too early to expect anything.'

'I hope you're right,' Richards muttered. 'By heaven, I hope you're right! I'll keep a constant check, and advise you how things go.'

'Splendid.' Denham nodded complacently. 'Do that. I'll be at home all evening, anyway.'

With that he left, not in the least concerned; but Richards was; very much so. He fled back to the power-room of C.

I. And watched the meters intently. An hour passed; then two hours, and there was no sign of a return to normal. Rather the reverse. '7' had gradually risen to '8' and the barometer had dropped several degrees. At last Richards could stand it no longer; he telephoned Denham and gave him the facts. To a certain extent Denham was shaken out of his complacent mood.

'I just don't understand it, Richards. Unless you've any suggestions? You're more closely in touch with the whole thing than I am.'

'I'm as baffled as you are, sir. We know the planes did their job and blasted the penitentiary, and therefore whatever disturbance might have been coming from there. There's only one possible answer — that we guessed wrong, and that the disturbance is coming from somewhere else. I'm wondering now if the Aurora Borealis has anything to do with it.'

'How could it have?'

'I can't say without working it out. There might be a magnetic connection somewhere which is causing the upset.'

'I doubt it. If it were so it would have

been evident long ago,' Denham sighed. 'Looks as if we destroyed a useful penitentiary for nothing ... Only one thing for it — explore the arctic region and see if there's anything to account for it.'

'Okay. When do we start?'

'How do you mean — 'we'?'

The scientist started. 'But you'll want to come too, surely?'

'Look, Richards, let's get one thing straight. I told you before I won't fly into the arctic tempest region for anybody; and anyway it's your job as chief scientist of C. I. Get out there and see what you can find. Take whom you like with you, and all the necessary instruments. Leave instructions with London-control to tell me of hourly readings on the instruments.'

'All right,' Richards growled. 'Do you want a television hook-up on closed circuit to see what happens to me?'

'Yes, might as well. Use channel 292.'

Denham rang off. He sat for a while in puzzled silence beside the telephone; then he got up and went to the big windows of his library. Everything seemed to be all right outside. The sky was soft blue, the air warm. Nowhere a cloud. Not far away across the grounds his son and a girl friend were playing tennis; in the nearer distance his wife was lounging in a garden seat, swinging herself gently to and fro as she read a novel.

'Queer,' Denham muttered. 'Damned queer. I wish I could understand it.'

For a moment he was a prey to underlying tensions, but he did not give way to them. He unlatched the window and looked out into the garden.

'I've got to stop here, Beryl,' he called to his wife. 'I'm watching the television as Richards takes a flight to the Arctic Circle.'

'What in the world's he doing that for?'

'On my orders. There's something queer going on with the weather. Don't disturb me unless you have to . . . '

Denham turned back into the library, lit a cigar, and then dumped himself into a comfortable armchair. Leaning forward, he switched the televisor to Channel 292 and then relaxed, watching the, as yet, motionless view transmitting from inside the fast jetplane that was going to be used for the Arctic trip. Now and again Richards himself came on. Carrying instruments — then came the other men whom he had selected to make the journey with him.

This went on for an hour, then the plane doors were closed and last minute preparations were made for the take-off. At the same moment the telephone rang. Denham took the instrument from its rest.

'Yes? Denham here.'

'London-control, sir. Hourly report as requested. Disturbance continues. Barometer fallen one degree. There seems now to be an added disturbance coming from the south. The south and north stations are disturbed in a degree of '9' and '6' respectively.'

'Thanks,' Denham said mechanically, staring in front of him. 'Report again in another hour.'

He put the phone down again and watched the televisor for a moment. The plane was in the air now, the television pick-up being so placed that it gave a view through the front observation window and the shoulders of Richards and his assistant to either side of the screen. From the view through the window the plane seemed to be streaking high over London, heading north.

Denham switched on the radio to short-wave closed circuit and livened the microphone.

'You receiving me, Richards? Over.'

'Receiving you. Mr. Denham,' Richards acknowledged. 'I'm heading north as requested, and Laycock is with me to run the instruments. Over.'

'I can see that from the television. I wanted to tell you that I've just had the first hourly report from London-control. The disturbance isn't getting better: it's worse. And now it's augmented by a strong influence from the south as well. It's getting quite beyond me. Any suggestions? Over.'

'None, sir. I just don't begin to understand it. Anyway, we'll see what the north tells us. If nothing, then we'll investigate to the south. Over and out.'

Denham switched off, watching for a

while the plane's fast progress out to the north of England, then beyond that to the sunny expanses of the Arctic Ocean. Here, on the one-time ice fringe, pleasure steamers sailed gaily in the brilliant sunlight. It was all so calm, so apparently undisturbed, that it gave the complete lie to the climatic station instruments. Yet they could not be wrong, as Denham well knew. Sooner or later something would show to account for the confusion of pressures.

The phone rang again. An hour had passed, and the position was unchanged. By this time the jet plane was nearing the sullen gray of the tempest regions, and the sunlight was dying — partly because of sunset and partly because of cloud. Denham watched the television screen intently, Richards and Laycock were silhouetted now against black swirling cloud and an observation window down which a deluge of rain was pouring. And with every moment they drove further and further into the eternal storm, the searchlights blazing forward and downward.

Denham leaned forward intently, watching every detail, the dead stump of his cigar between his teeth. As far as the bombed plateau was concerned, he could scarcely see it for the smother of rain and cloud . . . He reached to the radio, intent on asking a question — and at that identical moment the television screen blanked and became dead.

'What the devil . . . ?' Denham got out of his chair and fiddled with the instrument. It was working perfectly, a fact proven by the other channels coming instantly on the screen as he stabbed buttons — but he had definitely lost contact with Richards. By radio too. There was no answer.

Denham gave it up at last, swearing to himself. He wandered out onto the lawn and joined his wife, son, and young teenage tennis player.

Beryl Denham looked up in the warm twilight at her husband's face.

'Anything the matter, Marcus? You're not looking particularly happy.'

'With good reason. I've lost touch with the plane that was heading northwards.

Radio and television have gone dead. It was most essential that I keep in touch.'

'Probably a technical fault,' the younger Denham said. Then he seemed to think. 'What was the flight for, anyhow?'

'To check on — ' Denham made an impatient gesture as the phone rang in the library. 'Excuse me a moment.'

He hurried in to the instrument and whipped it up. 'Denham here. What is it?'

'London-control, sir.' The voice was agitated. 'Can you come at once? There's something happening which I don't like, and I don't feel qualified with Mr. Richards away. There's only you — '

'What's wrong now?' Denham snapped.

'It's the emergency-meter, sir. It's come into operation and is climbing steadily. There'll be disaster if we don't do something.'

'I'll come at once.' Denham slammed down the phone and darted to the window. 'Be back soon — emergency call,' he told his wife, and then he hurried off to get his car.

Beryl Denham did not have a chance to reply. In any case she had not taken much notice of her husband; she was suddenly conscious of how unnaturally still everything had become. Not a breath: not even a tremor of the leaves on the trees and bushes. It was the first dead-calm she had known since climatic control had been established.

In fifteen minutes Denham reached C. I. Headquarters and he went straight to the main power room. There, the deputy-chief was waiting for him, the measure of his anxiety obvious from the expression on his face.

'Well?' Denham asked briefly. 'What's wrong?'

'This, sir. Take a look — '

The engineer hurried along the main gangway with Denham close behind him. Before long they were facing the vast panel of dials, which Richards had studied so assiduously. The engineer pointed to one particularly large central dial, like an enormous clock face. It was graded into red-lined segments, and a needle was moving very slowly anti-clockwise across the segments towards the ultimate one which was clearly marked EXTREME DANGER.

'This, Mr. Denham, is the emergency meter, and it only comes into commission — '

'If extreme danger threatens,' Denham interjected. 'Dammit, man, I know that. I practically built this place myself — ' He stared at the needle's slow but relentless progress. 'This started just before you last rang me?'

'Yes. I haven't done anything about it. I thought I'd better wait for your instructions.'

Denham took off his jacket and tossed it onto the cowling of a nearby machine. Then he loosened his collar.

'We've a crisis on our hands,' he said abruptly. 'All the worse because we don't know what's causing it ... Somehow we've got to stop that needle rising otherwise the whole damned issue will blow up. Let's see what the other stations are doing.'

He swung actively to the radio, always connected with the other climatic machines. In a moment he was speaking to the controller of the Spitzbergen station.

'Denham here. Emergency meter in contact and rising on the London station. How are things with you?'

'Bad,' the engineer answered briefly. 'Emergency meter also operating here. It's reached 32, and the maximum's 50. If I don't cut out our station while the fault's traced we're in danger of exploding.'

'You'll not cut anything until I say so,' Denham snapped. 'The fault isn't in your station, or in London-control. It's in the atmosphere itself. An opposing atmospheric stream is being forced across our system from both north and south of the globe, but we'll beat it somehow. Stand by for further instructions.'

He switched off — then on again to the Bouvet Islands, the southernmost station. As the engineer in charge answered, Denham repeated the details he had given to Spitzbergen. The response did not cheer him much.

'Emergency reading of 40, sir. I don't know what's gone wrong, but when it gets near 50 we'll have to cut or go up in smoke.'

'You'll not cut till I say so.' Denham was sweating, his eyes on his own meter. The finger was crawling across the danger scale.

'I'm not waiting for your authority, Mr. Denham,' the southern engineer retorted. 'I'm in control of this station and I know danger when I see it. I'm not going to commit suicide for anybody.'

Denham breathed hard. 'Listen to me! If you cut out, the whole balance will be in jeopardy. You know that! You must not do it: I'll get this thing right — '

'Up to you. At 48 I cut, and I'm getting out quick with the others.'

Denham switched off, feeling very much like a man chained before the path of an advancing juggernaut. Courage he had in plenty, and he would fight anything he could see and understand — but how did one fight this? A creeping tide of extraneous atmospheric pressure from north and south which was gaining a hold every second. Though he could not understand how it was happening, he knew perfectly well that somehow two other climatic machines had been built and were working in opposition, apparently — as far as the northward one was concerned — unaffected by the nuclear bomb attack.

'Shall I — cut?' asked the deputy-chief, set-faced, as Denham tried to wrestle with the problem.

'No — Not yet! Let me think . . . We're at the mercy of outside pressures — the normal atmospheric drifts which we usually hold at bay with our machines — '

'We can't fight that kind of pressure,' the deputy said. 'We'd need every machine we've got going full belt, and even then we wouldn't do it. Things have advanced too far.'

Denham's eyes fixed on the emergency needle. It was just creeping over the 40-mark.

'Give me an order,' the deputy insisted, clutching Denham's arm. 'If you don't, I'll act for myself. I've got to, sir! The whole city will be in danger if this station blows up under the pressure.'

Denham took a deep breath. 'All right — cut out every machine and let the others manage as best they can. It may give us a brief respite in London here. Quickly!'

The engineer hesitated no longer. He snatched up a telephone and sent his orders to various parts of the great control-room, then he himself seized a master lever and pulled it sharply out of contact. The droning whine of vibratory machines ceased and whirred down into silence. Instantly the emergency indicator dropped to zero — but only because power had ceased to flow into it.

Silence. Denham wiped perspiration from his face with the back of his sleeve. The radio buzzed for attention. He turned and switched it on.

'Denham speaking. London-control.'

'Spitzbergen station, sir. I can't hold out any more. The emergency indicator registers 49 and — '

Suddenly the voice ceased and in the speaker there came an overwhelming crash and then silence. Denham looked up to meet the deputy's grim eyes.

'Looks as though the Spitzbergen station has gone for good, sir.'

Denham nodded, almost stupidly. 'It's

— it's only to be expected. Now we've cut our load they'll step theirs up, which will bring them more quickly to disaster. But there was nothing we could do. Nothing.'

The deputy asked: 'What do we do now? If all the stations go?'

'I don't know. Have to see what happens . . . I'll go up to my office and work something out. Keep me in touch.'

'Yes, sir.'

Denham turned and went slowly down the gangway, bewildered by events. He hardly remembered arriving at his office. Switching on the light, he went over to his swivel chair and sat down. Then he stared in front of him, still wrestling mentally with the problem. He was sure there ought to be an answer, but none came.

Finally he got to his feet again and opened the window. The air in the office seemed intolerably close, despite the fact that he was still in shirtsleeves. He stood for a while gazing at the lights of the city. Everything seemed intensely calm and still: it did not seem to have made any difference shutting off the London-control machine.

'Mr. Denham . . . '

He turned, starting. He had not heard the door open. The deputy chief was standing by the desk, his face pale.

'I'm afraid we're in for trouble, Mr. Denham.'

'I rather expected we would be.' Denham smiled bitterly. 'What's the latest news?'

'Bad — all of it. None of the stations reply except the one in Northern Canada. They report that their particular station will be at maximum danger position any moment and they're evacuating. They also report rapid cloud drift from the north. I've picked up radio reports from the principal cities and they all tell of the collapse of weather control. Some report earthquakes, others floods and tornadoes. There's a great belt of violently disturbed conditions sweeping down from the north. We can't hope to sidestep it . . . I think I should warn the public, Mr. Denham. They might be able to protect themselves. Climatic control's gone — for the time being, anyway.'

'Yes,' Denham muttered. 'Yes, I'll tell

the public . . . Thanks for the information.'

The deputy went out and Denham looked at the radio. It was up to him to sign his own death warrant — to tell the public that climatic control had broken down and that disastrous disturbances were on the way, were already battering the northern half of the world and advancing at unknown speed.

Denham looked again through the window. The stars were still glinting in the still sky. The air was motionless. The last shreds of climatic control were still functioning.

'Why tell them and cut my own throat?' Denham asked himself, half aloud. 'Afterwards there may still be time to get things right . . . '

'There'll never be time for that, Denham!'

Denham swung, open-mouthed. As on the other occasion, he had not heard the door open. For that matter, the deputy engineer had not shut it completely after him; he'd been in too much of a hurry for that . . . Now a tall man in a leather flying-jacket was advancing toward the desk, the glint of murder in his eyes.

'David Brook!' Denham gasped, staring. 'It — it can't be!'

9

When the Earth shook

'It can be, and it is!' David said, reaching the desk. 'It took more than the Arctic penitentiary to hold me. I warned you about that, remember? I said I'd come back — and now I've done it.'

Denham moved slowly. 'How? How did you do it?'

'I'll sum everything up in a few words, Denham. I came back to settle accounts with you — to settle up for my father, my mother, my fiancée and myself. You're beaten, Denham, and everybody's against you, even the innocent 'criminals' you've had incarcerated in Arctic and Antarctic.'

Denham gestured, even tried a rather unconvincing smile. 'All right, so you've escaped. You know the regulations. Escape from one of the polar prisons means that the escapee is free to resume his life in society. That's how it will be with you. No questions asked. You can come back.'

'Very magnanimous of you.' The cold glint in David's eyes was somehow frightening. 'And, incidentally, that's a regulation I never heard of, conveniently invented on the spur of the moment because you're afraid of what's going to happen.'

Denham moved again and sat rather shakily in his chair. He fumbled for a cigar, stuck it in his mouth, but did not light it. His blue eyes fixed on David's expressionless face.

'Do we look at each other for the rest of the night?' Denham asked at last, controlling himself. 'You're a man of action, that's evident — and so am I. Therefore — '

'Shut up!' David interrupted. 'And keep shut up while I tell you a few things. First, climatic control is ended because opposition machines are at work at both Poles. You made an attempt to wreck the Arctic machine, as I thought you would — and you made a good job of destroying

242

the Arctic pen. Only there was nobody in the place, and no machinery either. You were outsmarted, Denham.'

Denham said nothing. He lighted his cigar and waited. The heat seemed stifling again, even though the window was wide open to the stillness of the night.

'The inmates of the pen moved out to natural caves,' David went on. 'Caves that were part of the plateau itself, and some distance from the site of the pen. It was easy to do that since deep underground excavations had been made for the prison extensions. Down there the opposition machine was built. I saw to that. Every detail, remembered from the plans and notes made by my father . . . When your bombers came along they simply shook things as far as we were concerned — and nothing more. We were protected by rock from blast and shock waves. We had all the power we needed to work our generators — power from the tempest-driven ocean itself . . . You still listening, Denham?'

Denham smiled sourly. 'You told me to shut up until you'd finished talking. I have to congratulate you on several smart moves.'

'You can keep your congratulations: I don't want them . . . After the bombing raid we gave instructions to the Antarctic Pen to release their machine as well, thereby completing our plan. It was all done by transport planes and willing cooperation, born of hatred of you, Denham, and your tin-pot climatic dictatorship. We had it all arranged to escape in transport planes only, in my case, there was a lucky chance — You sent a batch of scientists to investigate the Arctic conditions.'

'My chief scientist and his assistant. I suppose you shot them down, or something?'

'Nobody shot them down. They crashed in the Arctic storms. If you knew their fury you wouldn't be surprised at that. It was a wonder your bombing fleet came through as it did . . . However, they crashed. The two men and the pilot were killed by the impact but the plane itself was not too badly damaged. We saw the incident, went to the spot, and got the plane airworthy again. I used it myself to come here. Being a pilot of considerable experience I managed to dodge the storm centers. The rest of the Pen inmates will either use transport planes, sent by willing cooperation, or else they'll stay in hiding until the disturbances of disturbed climate are over.'

Denham did not speak. His ear was cocked to a curious rumbling sound outside. Probably heavy traffic, or else far distant thunder.

'Getting in here was simple enough,' David concluded, shrugging. 'I haven't got prison garb, thanks to using the clothes of one of the men in the plane. There's no law against coming up to your office, so the hall commissionaire didn't stop me . . . It's all quite simple, really.'

'And melodramatic,' Denham commented, knocking the ash from his cigar into the brass ashtray. 'Well, what next? Now you've managed to wreck the climatic machines and return to safety, what happens?'

'To safety?' David shook his head. 'I've returned to a bigger hell than you imagine. By this time all your subsidiary machines have either exploded or been overwhelmed by the advancing tide of natural air currents. Those currents are going to sweep the globe and create terrific disturbances as they form once again into normal paths. So far London hasn't been touched, but it will be — then it will be every man for himself. Before that happens, I want some information from you.'

'What?'

'Where do I find Ruth Dornsey?'

Denham hesitated, then the look in David's eyes destroyed his reticence. 'In the fourth women's labor corps.'

'Where do I find their headquarters? And don't try to pull anything, Denham. If you tell me a lie, I'll come back and get the truth.'

'It's located at the corner of Two and Six intersection in the city center. You can see the position from the window here.'

Denham got to his feet and went across the office. David followed him, then as he reached the window, the tycoon suddenly grabbed him by the throat, forcing him by sheer bull-like strength toward the open window. David was caught by surprise. He tumbled off balance toward the low frame, and he might even have gone sailing through it toward the city lights far below had a sudden tremendous concussion not upset Denham's calculations.

It was more than a concussion: it was a gulping and straining of the Earth itself, accompanied by an ever-increasing, rumbling growl. The floor shook, sending both Denham and David reeling back into the office. Glass splintered, window frames buckled, and the big light globe in the ceiling began to swing back and forth like a pendulum.

'Earthquake,' Denham panted, releasing David abruptly. 'That's what it is, isn't it?'

David did not answer. Instead he drew back his fist and then slammed it home with all the force of his hard young muscles. Back of the blow was all the resentment and fury he had been penning back. He watched Denham stagger backwards, slither over the big desk, and crash beyond it to the floor — then David was out of the office and in the corridor, his mind centered now on only one thing. He had got to find Ruth Dornsey, and quickly, before earthquake and climatic upheaval brought the city to ruin.

He had got as far as the elevator when the second shock came. The floor swayed crazily and fissures ripped up the walls with the noise of a dozen guns. The lights went out. In the darkness there was a tumult of sounds — falling masonry, hoarse shouts, the clang of alarm bells. David clutched the trembling wall and looked about him. He saw the staircase and dived for it, his way lighted by a blinding flash of lightning.

With the noise of thunder and earth-tremor dinning in his ears he raced down flight after flight of stairs, dodging and pushing his way through a milling crowd of panic-stricken employees. In the lower reaches of the vast building the confusion was absolute. Darkness, and the failure of the emergency lighting only added to the chaos. From experience, David knew where the main hallway door was, and somehow he fought his way to it through struggling, shouting men and women.

As he passed through it there came another tremor. It flung David helplessly down the steps of the building. He crashed on his back, wincing with pain. Lightning seared the sky at the same moment and his wide-open eyes beheld an unbelievable and terrifying sight. The huge central mass of the C.I. building, with Denham's office at the top of it, was leaning far outwards, toppling — toppling —

David scrambled to his feet as the darkness shut down again. He ran — and ran — It didn't matter where as long as he got free of the falling building. Rain suddenly smote him in a deluge as he floundered on. Behind him the central face of the C.I. edifice thundered to the ground in an avalanche of masonry and steel. The thick, sultry air was abruptly pierced by frantic screams.

David slowed to a halt. He had missed the collapse of the building front so there was no need to run any more. But he had to find Ruth — somehow. Bewildered, he looked about him. Rain was streaming down in solid sheets, pouring into the cracks and gulfs of what had been the main street. The incessant lightning revealed piled-up traffic, some of it tumbling into the chasms, other parts of it flung in all directions as though a giant's hammer had struck it.

How did one find Labor Camp Four in *this*? All signposts had gone. The whole city had been shaken out of recognition by the earthquake. There were mountains of rubble to be traversed. David groaned to himself and shook the rain out of his eyes ... Then again the screams from rearward attracted his attention. Help was desperately needed, and at the moment he was in the best position to give it.

He swung round and raced back to the mountains of debris. Already there were hundreds of rescuers at work, men and women from the C.I. building who had escaped the general collapse, but even so there was more work than they could handle. David, his way illumined by the lightning, climbed a mountain of rain-slippery masonry and dropped to the other side. He caught a glimpse of men and women, pinned by the avalanche. He started towards them and then paused, staring. He couldn't be sure but —

Now he was certain. A dazzling flash of lightning revealed it again. A jagged trench in the earth, built up on two sides by vast mountains of rubble. But in the trench were two skeletons.

David stopped, thoughts hammering into his mind. The cries of the injured, the din of the storm, the threat of new collapses from the doomed building, did not mean a thing. They were in another world. Two skeletons? Obviously they must have belonged to bodies buried long before the present cataclysm.

A party of rescuers came stumbling by, relieving David of the responsibility he had been going to shoulder. The injured ones in the vicinity were going to be taken care of . . .

Skeletons? He went forward at last, everything nakedly clear in the blue and sizzling flashes from the tortured skies. He got to the skeletons finally and stood staring at them deep in the trench. The trench was neat and perfectly cut. It had probably housed a wall before the collapse . . .

In the wind an oblong piece of paper began to move, stirred from the ribs of the bigger skeleton. David dived for it, seized it, and started to unfold it. As he did so he looked into the trench. There was a wallet there, with part of the contents spewed out.

He opened the oblong paper slowly. It had already become sodden with rain. Dirt smeared with the rain and left streaks that hid the typing beneath. But David saw enough . . . It was an agreement, and the names of Alvin Brook and Marcus Denham were evident. There was even a date, ten years old.

Thunder belched and slammed across the sky as David stood there quivering. He jumped down into the trench and snatched up the wallet. He hardly needed to examine it: he remembered it. His father's — with his mother's photograph still in its place behind a celluloid front panel.

Abruptly, the real horror of the

situation struck home to David. The wallet tumbled out of his quivering hands. He knew now whose skeletons these were. Originally the bodies must have been behind a party wall or something — Oh, what did it matter? For a moment or two he didn't care any more. He crouched in the trench, fast filling with water, and fumbled with quivering hands for any other relics that might be there. He found one — an earring with an imitation emerald. As it lay in his palm he remembered. It had belonged, with its fellow, to his mother. He himself had given her the earrings for a birthday present . . .

Suddenly David found himself crying. It was the only possible way in which his mind could find relief. And he kept on crying until danger signals around him insisted on being noticed. For one thing the trench was fast flooding; for another, the rising gale was sweeping chunks of masonry out of the shattered C.I. building, chunks which would hit him if he didn't move quickly.

Forced to realities, he jumped out of

the trench and then proceeded to claw his way over the greasy masses of stone and twisted metal. He encountered rescuers coming in the opposite direction but he paid no attention to them — or they to him . . . Back of his mind now there was only a single thought: he had got to try and find Ruth, somehow. In the matter of more local rescue there was nothing he could do.

He slid down the remaining mass of masonry to the ruins of the street, and met the full force of the hurricane that had broken loose. It carried sharp stinging stones before it; it bent double those few people who were struggling against it. It moaned and roared with ever increasing violence through the earthquake-shattered ruins of buildings. Doggedly, David battled against it, the lightning showing him where to go, the rain lashing in solid sheets against him.

Through the blur ahead he could roughly make out the position of the intersection at Two and Six, a square with which he was fairly familiar from experience, but between him and his goal were shattered buildings, blaring ambulances, fallen pedestrian ways, and an insane tangle of overhead power wires . . . He came to a stop, breathless, as the wind increased its fury and strove mightily to tear him from his feet.

As he stood thus, his back to the hurricane, his eyes fixed on two blinding lights coming towards him. A car-horn blared savagely, driving out of the way the scurrying men and women, and even causing an ambulance to swerve perilously into a mass of rubble to avoid collision.

'He's either blind or incredibly selfish,' David muttered, moving out of the somewhat clearer region that ran down the center of the main street. 'Pity somebody doesn't teach him a lesson — '

He dived for safety as the car bore down on him, horn blasting a devil's wail. David stared as the car swept by, bouncing over stones and chippings, its normal immense power checked somewhat by the force of the wind . . . Lightning ripped the sky again, and David gave a start. He saw the driver for a split second

— Marcus Denham himself, in shirtsleeves, blood-streaked and filthy, plainly throwing everything into an effort to drive through the city. Actually Denham was trying to get home, but David was not of course aware of it.

David moved — and quickly. He fought through the hurricane's retarding power, racing after the car like a madman, and because the wind and confusion was so vast Denham could not put on any speed. Indeed, he stopped entirely as a boulder, across his path, loomed into view. That was David's chance. Fighting the wind he came to the car's side and snatched open the door. Denham stared at him fixedly, more lightning vividly illuminating the big cut on his forehead.

He only stared for a moment, then his hand dived for something he evidently had ready on the dashboard shelf — but he had no chance to use it. David reached inside, grabbed him by an arm and neck, and pulled with all his strength. Denham, cursing and gasping, slithered along the big upholstered seat and crashed on his back amid the stones. He gave a cry of pain as sharp edges bit through his thin shirt.

'Maybe the account isn't quite settled, Denham!' David stood over him, legs straddled and back bent against the wind. 'I thought you'd been wiped out when the C.I. building collapsed, but evidently I was wrong.'

'I got away in time,' Denham panted, struggling up, his shirt plastered to his flabby chest. 'Have sense, Brook! The only thing that matters is that we should get clear of this hell! Come on — I'll give you a lift. We can manage it in the car.'

'By knocking everybody else out of the way we might — but I don't favor those tactics. I've something to settle with you.' David paused as thunder drowned his words for a moment. 'I just came across two skeletons, and there's not a shadow of doubt whose bodies they were once.'

'Dammit, man, be sensible!' Denham screamed, as behind him the C.I. building finally succumbed to a bolt of lightning. 'We can't talk here.'

'We can and we're going — ' David got no further. He had not seen the chunk of masonry Denham had whipped up in a brief interval of darkness. It whirled and David staggered as it struck the top of his head. He dropped to his knees, dazed, but not entirely stunned.

The deluging rain revived him. He shook his head savagely to clear the blur before his eyes, and was in time to see Denham's gross, saturated figure scrambling away over the massive stones at the side of the road. Immediately David started to follow — then he checked himself. By so doing he avoided the collapse of one of the biggest boulders as it came crashing down with the force of several tons straight onto the rubble across which Denham was battling. There was one brief scream, then the boulders came together with shattering impact as a thunderclap cannoned out of the sky.

David breathed hard and passed a hand over his aching, rain-soaked head. The end of Denham had come so suddenly he hardy realized it even now. He felt almost cheated out of his personal revenge — Then the ground heaved again and warned him that danger was still all around him. Not yet was the fury of returning normal climate over.

The earth-shock this time was not a severe one, but it brought the parts of the city still standing completely down. The main menace now was the wind, screaming at something like 100 miles an hour through the chaos. Fortunately it reached its peak velocity only in gusts, so little by little David was able to make his soaked and dazzled way forward.

The more he progressed into the heart of the city the more he realized how enormous was the damage. Hardly a building stood complete, and those which did had gaping sockets for windows and the doors had been wrenched off. But in amidst the flood, wind, and lashing rain men and women still moved, each with a purpose, each determined somehow to survive the chaos to which they were being subjected.

So, through a maze of rubbish that had once been a main street, David came finally to the Inter-section of Two and Six — and stared appalled. There was not a building standing, and the Women's

Labor Corps Building — the situation of which he was vaguely familiar — was nothing but a big mass of broken stone, fast being engulfed in the waters pouring more profusely through the city.

A woman came hurrying past in a torn uniform. David made a grab at her. She turned a white, startled face in the glare of lightning.

'Sorry,' David apologized. 'Maybe you can help me — Do you belong to the Labor Corps?'

'No — the Women's Auxiliary. Hurry please: I've an emergency on my hands.'

'Do you know what's happened to the Women's Labor Corps now their building has been shattered?' David bellowed his words over the wind and thunder.

'No idea.' The woman was already going away. 'The earthquake brought the building down. I saw it happen. I suppose the women would be buried underneath . . .'

She was gone. David turned stupidly and looked at the small mountain of rubble and stone that had been the building. For a moment he was full of thoughts of digging into the debris, then common sense prevailed. There were several tons of rubbish to be moved, and even if it could be done there could hardly be anybody alive under that pressing weight of stone and steel.

'Forget it,' David muttered to himself. 'That sort of thing pays no divi- dends . . . '

He began moving again, a drenched and wind-battered figure. He did not particularly care where he went, or what he did. Men and women passed him, struggling like himself, against the ele- ments, and for the most part he ignored them, until presently he came upon a rescue squad.

'We could do with you,' the leader shouted, a drenched and massively built man with a rope coil on his shoulders. 'We need every man we can get on the rescue team — Unless you're on an urgent mission.'

'No.' David shrugged. 'There isn't anything that's urgent for me anymore. I'll help.'

'Good man — follow us.'

David promptly fell in with the team. The company cheered his flagging spirits. The elements did not seem too big a problem when there were others in the same predicament as himself. He helped in the rescue work throughout the night, going to various parts of the wrecked and flooded city, helping to get the injured away to makeshift hospitals, and the dead to an enormous communal grave not far from the razed C.I. Building.

So busy was he, David had not much time to notice what was going on around him — but even he became aware that, after many hours of backbreaking work in the ruins, the fury of the storm was abating. The lightning was ceasing; the thunder grew more remote, and the hurricane abated to a stiff breeze. When the first ragged streaks of the day were showing there was a stiff, fresh breeze and a steady downpour pattering on the broken stones and metalwork that had been buildings the night before.

'It seems to me,' said the big fellow, who had been carrying a rope, 'that we've done all we can for the moment. When the rain lets up we can look further, but we've got out practically everybody in our particular area. Besides, there's a limit to endurance. I'm damned tired, and I'm pretty sure you must be.'

'Yes, I could do with a rest, 'David admitted. 'To say nothing of a meal and the chance to get dried out.'

'You can have all that at one of the emergency rest-centers. Come with me. There's free clothes and meals for rescue teams.'

David didn't argue. He followed the big fellow through the crowded city center, past endless little communities trying to shape some sort of comfort amidst the ruin and flood, and came finally to an enormous, hastily erected covered area where men and women in hundreds were resting, sleeping, drying-out, or talking to one another. Roughly though the great shelter had been constructed, it was nevertheless more or less proof against the steady rain, though in a deluge it would not stand a chance.

David did not worry over these possibilities: he had had enough horror crowded into him already. Anything else in prospect seemed footling by comparison. With the big fellow as his guide he joined the queue for soup and bread, collected a bundle of dry clothes supplied from a ruined store that had escaped flood damage, and then settled down thankfully before a hastily contrived oil stove. The soup he consumed as he was, in his torn and dripping clothes — then he went to the relative privacy of a ruck-sacked corner, put on the too big outfit that had been provided, and returned to the oil stove to rest. The big fellow, also in a dry outfit, came through the thronging men and women and settled beside him. He proffered some bent but quite dry cigarettes.

'Thanks.' David took one, lighted it at the stove, and inhaled gratefully. 'Just what I needed . . . '

They were quiet for a moment, both of them looking at the increasing daylight behind a ragged silhouette of broken buildings. There was even a streak of pale blue sky far down in the east.

'Lost anybody, friend?' the big fellow asked suddenly.

'Yes . . . My fiancée.'

'Sorry — really I am.' An enormous hand patted David's knee in sympathy. 'I've been pretty fortunate. My wife and two children are safe. Hurt a bit, but nothing serious. I've been lucky. There must have been thousands killed in this lot, and as many thousands bereaved . . . I don't rightly understand what caused it all. Last night it was perfect — not a breath. Then suddenly this catastrophe descends on us . . . must be the result of monkeying about with the weather. Nature never intended we should try to do it, in spite of the line Marcus Denham handed us about the genius of man taming the blind force of Nature.'

David smiled faintly. 'It was in the wrong hands. Climatic control is a marvelous conception, but it should not be in the hands of one controlling clique. An international body ought to control it. That way, everybody would be satisfied.'

'Perhaps . . . ' The big man reflected, then shook his head. 'I don't know, though. After last night . . . I don't think control of the climate will ever catch on again. Besides, those who ran it are probably dead. The secret's gone, and it may be centuries before it's rediscovered.'

'I don't think so,' David said quietly, but he did not add to his remark. He had not been intending to, anyway, but as it was all thought of conversation vanished for a moment as he absently studied a distant queue of ragged, weary women waiting for soup. Just for a moment he thought he —

'Would you excuse me?' he asked abruptly; then jumping to his feet he plunged into the crowd.

He had some difficulty in forcing his way, mainly because the women thought he was trying to jump their queue — but finally he succeeded, diving after one woman in particular as he caught up with her. She swung, then dropped the soup in sheer amazement.

'Dave!' she gasped hoarsely. 'Oh, Dave — '

David had her in his arms immediately, kissing her face fervently, looking at her intently, then kissing her again. He had not been mistaken. Dirty and ragged though she was, the girl was still Ruth Dornsey.

'Thank God I found you,' David whispered, as their emotion cooled a little. 'I was told every woman had been killed in the collapse of the Corps building. Then I — '

'I was out on rescue work when the collapse came,' Ruth interrupted. 'I've been helping in rescue work — But you! How do you come to be here? I thought you were in the Arctic Penitentiary.'

'It's a long story. I'll tell you about it over your meal — Come back and get another lot. Better still, I'll get it, or they may think you're trying to get a ration twice over. And don't move from this spot! Don't!'

'I won't!' Ruth promised, watching with eager eyes as David went back into the queue. In ten minutes he was back again with another bowl of soup and some more bread. Ruth fell into step beside him as they made for the crowded rest center.

'It's like a miracle,' Ruth said. 'Your being here, I mean. Honest, I never expected to see you again.'

'No more than I expected to see you, after last night and the collapse of the Corps building — Here's a place to sit. Now have your soup and talk as you do it.'

They squatted down on two upturned boxes, oblivious to the chatter of men and women around them. The whole center was alive with the excited conversation of reunion.

'There's not really much to tell,' Ruth said, between mouthfuls of soup. 'I got detailed onto rescue work, and a bolt of lightning hit the Corps building while I was out on the job. I kept at it until dawn, then I was just too exhausted to go any further. I went to a food queue — and there it is.'

'Your clothes are wet,' David said seriously, studying her. 'You ought to have got a dry bundle when you got your food . . . I'll do it while you eat. Don't move from here.'

He went off quickly. When he returned

Ruth had finished her soup and bread and was gazing speculatively at the yellow gold of the sunrise peeping through the eastern stretch of blue. She glanced up as she realized David was beside her.

'Get changed,' he said briefly, handing her the bundle of clothing. 'That's the spot over there. It's private enough.'

She nodded and went over to the corner rendered private by the enormous stretched rucksack. David smiled to himself and sat down on his box. Suddenly, he was at peace with the world — at peace for the first time in his life. It seemed strange really, to be at peace in the ruins of a city surrounded by nothing but utter confusion. Yet perhaps his mood was not so very remarkable. Ruth was back alive and well — that was the main thing. And Denham had ceased to exist: that was the other factor. The two dreams of his life had abruptly come true.

How long he sat meditating and watching the dawn really break through he had no idea. He only came back to earth as he realized that Ruth was there again, sliding down onto the upturned box. She had cleaned her face somewhat and tried to fasten her hair back. David gave an appreciative smile and looked at her more attentively. Even so weariness from her night's rescue work was obvious, and underlying that again were the lines and hollows born of her year in the labor Corps. In that moment David was glad Denham was dead; he even had a momentary exultation in the thought that he had died horribly, beneath the overwhelming weight of the boulder.

'Better now?' David asked gently, taking the girl's coarsened hand.

'I'm with you,' she answered simply. 'There's no other answer needed is there?'

'Dearest . . . ' David looked into her sincere gray eyes for a moment, then the girl's next remark rather startled him.

'What do you suppose is going to happen to us, David? I have still two years to go in the Labor Corps and you have escaped from the penitentiary. Will we — be sent back?'

'No — never that again. We're free. Right at the beginning of something new.

All the regulations were made by Marcus Denham, and he's dead. I saw him die.'

'You did? Last night, you mean?'

David gave her the details. When he had finished the sun had broken through and was pouring an intense heat on to the pools and mud of the night. Steam began to rise in drifting clouds.

'In effect, then,' Ruth said slowly, 'you caused all the havoc last night?'

'Indirectly, I suppose I did. It was either that or let the world go on being governed by a monstrous injustice and a stolen idea. There couldn't help but be havoc when things reverted to normal. I make no apology; I did nothing murderous. I only gave the order for release of counter-machines, which I built from my father's own specification. It destroyed Denham, and so exacted justice for his own murderous tactics. If things had been left as they were, injustice would have grown and flourished. Desperate ills need desperate remedies, Ruth, and I'm not ashamed of what I did. I saw a foul evil flourishing, and so destroyed it. There was no other way.'

'No,' Ruth admitted quietly. 'There was no other way.'

'You don't hold it against me?'

'I can only say that, had I been governed by the same motives as yourself, I would probably have done the same thing.'

'Probably?' David repeated.

'I'm a woman, Dave — and that makes a difference. I can't altogether assess it from your angle. I don't suppose the women of the world ever have been able to. The men make the wars, the tragedies, and the triumphs. The women just follow behind them because there's nothing else they can do.'

There was a long silence. The sunlight had increased its brightness as the clouds of the night's catastrophe began to break up into enormous gulfs of blue sky.

'What's going to happen?' Ruth asked at last. 'Everything has changed back again after last night. The old order has value again, and the new one — which came with climatic control — does not mean a thing. Are you going to carry on where Denham left off as far as the climate is concerned?'

David shook his head. 'No. I'm going to try and forget Denham, as most other people will try to do. As for climatic control — Well, perhaps some day. I want to get back into the air force. I want to build a home for both of us — and above all I want time to think about dad's invention. If climatic control comes back it will have to be with sanity.'

Ruth laid a hand on his arm. 'Sanity and climatic control will always be uneasy bedfellows, Dave. There will always be Denhams in the world, and it will take a stronger man than you to master them. Why not leave things as they are? Leave at least one possession to outraged Nature and let her handle it?'

Dave said nothing. He smiled and put his arm about the girl's shoulders. He knew at heart that she was right.

We do hope that you have enjoyed reading this large print book.

Did you know that all of our titles are available for purchase?

We publish a wide range of high quality large print books including:
Romances, Mysteries, Classics
General Fiction
Non Fiction and Westerns

Special interest titles available in large print are:
The Little Oxford Dictionary
Music Book, Song Book
Hymn Book, Service Book

Also available from us courtesy of Oxford University Press:
Young Readers' Dictionary
(large print edition)
Young Readers' Thesaurus
(large print edition)

For further information or a free brochure, please contact us at:
Ulverscroft Large Print Books Ltd.,
The Green, Bradgate Road, Anstey,
Leicester, LE7 7FU, England.
Tel: (00 44) **0116 236 4325**
Fax: (00 44) **0116 234 0205**